BABY COME BACK

CHERYL BARTON

Thank you!

In honor of those who enjoy my books and have been fans of mine on this journey, here is a love story that gets right to it without a whole lot of fluff. Preston Washington wanted his woman back and when he was ready, he set out to do that by any means necessary. Fall in love with him as he goes in search of his heart that he left behind with the woman who was and still is his everything.

Thank you for riding with me all this time. There is much more to come!

I appreciate you!

Let's discover love again and again, together!

Dedication

To a friend's son, Preston, who lost a battle to cancer four years ago. I have main characters in two of my books who are named Preston in his honor because his mother is a fan who has supported me as an author since my first book. She also shared how my stories have helped her smile through her darkest days. I thank you!

Stand Alone Romance
Snowbound
Cupid's Arrow
One Wish
His Halloween Promise
Holly for Christmas
A Better Man
Bossy
Un-Break My Heart
Love on Top
Take a Knee
Love at First Sight
My First Love
Black Love
A Younger Man
The Lake House
True Lies or True Love
When I Think of You
Baby, Come Back
Unforgettable

1
Three Years Ago

"Prez, I still can't believe you did all of this for me. How could you afford this?"

Sumaria Moore admirably took in the large majestic appearance of the oceanfront Miami, Florida hotel suite overlooking the Atlantic Ocean and wondered how she'd gotten this lucky. She was in the perfect place with the perfect man just days after her graduation from Florida State University with a dual degree in Interior Design and Finance. She was proud to have presented her degree to her mother and father, Bernard and Sylvia Moore, who made sure her desire to go to college and come out with two degrees came to fruition. The icing on the cake, that was the day of her graduation, was when she looked up amongst the hundreds of other graduates all in line and excited about the upcoming ceremony and saw the love of her life since she was fifteen years old, Preston

Washington, whom she called Prez, walking proudly up to her with an armful of roses just as the processional in was about to begin. She wasn't sure he would make it from their hometown, Meridian, Mississippi, all the way to Tallahassee, Florida, knowing how tight money was for him and his pride often got in the way when she offered to help him financially. Today, he had come through and not only shown up, but also whisked her away for the perfect weekend.

She couldn't believe she'd woken up with a view so perfect that it practically took her breath away. They had arrived at the hotel the night before, after spending time with her parents after the ceremony at a dinner where the four of them sat celebrating her and talked about her plans now that school was done.

When the hour turned late and her parents began the drive back to Meridian, she and Preston prepared to make the next few days alone as magical as possible.

It couldn't have been easy for him to do all of this when keeping a steady job was complicated for him. This wasn't just a hotel room, it was a suite and had to have cost him a pretty penny. That penny wasn't easy to come by when the kind of work available to him was nothing like the dreams of being a writer and producer of music that he'd had since he was a little boy.

The suite had so many personal touches, she didn't know what to focus on first. Preston had somehow wrangled up several vases of flowers spread throughout the sitting area and the bedroom and what she loved most of all were the many balloons in a rainbow of colors across the ceiling and covering sections of the floor. How he got it all done, she didn't know, but she loved him even more for it.

"Anything for you and you know that," he replied from the other room, outside of the bedroom where he asked her to wait before she came out. "The hotel just delivered our dinner, so come eat. I have a lot I want to talk to you about," he yelled.

With child-like excitement, she exited the bedroom, still in her black satin nightie and tiptoed across the thick brown carpet in her bare feet as she gazed wide-eyed at the full spread of food in front of her. She was glad she had followed his request that she pack for a few days before allowing her father to take everything back to Meridian from her off-campus apartment where she'd lived with her best friend, Tara, since their junior year. Knowing she and Preston didn't get a lot of time alone together, she wasn't surprised that they'd spent the night before and most of the day in bed and she'd brought more than a few sexy things to wear just for his viewing pleasure.

"Now, you're just showing off," she declared.

"Baby, this is a big moment in your life and I wanted to show you how much I appreciate and love you and how proud of you I am for all that you have accomplished. My baby is a college graduate and that's major," Preston shouted.

She loved their love. Who knew she'd find the love

of her life at fifteen years old and nine years later, they would still be together?

"I'm glad you were able to get here for the graduation. When my mom said you weren't riding with them, I was afraid something had happened."

When she tried to look under the heavy silver food covers, she giggled when he pushed her hand away. She loved being surprised, but she hated the suspense of the moment.

"I know and I'm sorry about that. My crazy boss at the store asked me to do one last furniture run from the warehouse and I didn't want to make your parents late. The guy is so miserable that he hates when anyone else is happy. He knew I was planning this trip to your graduation and he tried to mess it up. I can't wait until I no longer have to work for anyone. Anyway, on the train here, my cell phone wasn't working and I didn't know you were trying to reach me until I arrived and got off the train. By then, I was late and I needed to get the hotel room and some other stuff done to surprise you. I'm sorry if you thought I wouldn't be here for your big day. I never would have missed this."

Hands, lips and arms – she felt them all as he pulled her close to him, her favorite place to be. With her a twenty-four and him at twenty-six, their love was everything. Not many of her friends or even her parents thought they'd still be together since they seemed to be so opposite, but for her, it was all in how he treated her and with so little to his name, he was able to give her the most important thing; his heart.

Going into Prez's outstretched arms, she pressed her face to his bare chest, unable to imagine a more perfect moment. From the moment they met over nine years ago in high school when she was in the tenth grade and he was in the eleventh, no one meant more to her or made her feel like she could do anything like he did for her. He was her rock and she was his, even through the craziness that was his life, a far contrast from hers.

"I know. I was worried, that's all, but you made it up to me when you handed me the flowers. I couldn't stop smelling them throughout the ceremony and every time I looked over, you were smiling from ear to ear at me."

The quick, sweet kiss to her neck drew her mind back to how slow and sexy they had come together as one the night before. They'd had sex many times since their first time after her senior prom, but the night before, she knew it was more than that; it was lovemaking in its most passionate and zealous form.

"I'm just glad that I can support you the way you've always supported and looked out for me. I know it hasn't been easy with me and the mess that is my life, but you've been here and that means everything."

"It's all so amazing!"

Sumaria cheered as Preston walked around the set table, something he wouldn't let her see until this very moment. She'd been in the bedroom of the suite, relaxing until he told her it was time to come out. Taking a moment to appreciate what he's done, she saw before her a round table covered in a gold, satin table cloth. There was real china, and not just paper products and real silverware. In the center of the table sat a bottle of Moscato, her favorite drink, chilling on ice. There were red and white flower petals all over the table and even throughout the open space on the floor. Soft music played from his cell phone which was prominently set up on a side table facing where they would be eating. Looking over at him with love in her heart and in her eyes, she loved him with everything in her and most of all, she loved their love. Preston was not only handsome and sexy, but thoughtful and caring and when they were together, she had all of his attention.

"I told you I was going to plan something nice for you," he said.

"You outdid yourself," she said as he began showing her the food. She clapped with glee when she saw some of her favorite things.

"Stuffed salmon! Is that crabmeat inside of it?" she beamed.

"It certainly is."

She snickered when he beat on his chest like Tarzan, proud of himself, as he should be.

"I see steamed crab legs, grilled shrimp, steak medallions with onions and mushrooms, green beans, Caesar salad, vegetable rice and no you didn't!" she screamed.

Playing innocent, she swatted Preston playfully when she saw how he'd gone above and beyond her expectation with her most favorite sugary dessert.

"Oh, yes I did. You know this would not be a meal without it."

Sumaria leaned over the table and inhaled the aroma of her favorite, strawberry cheesecake. Unable to resist, she swiped her finger across the creaminess and the moment it touched her lips, all was right in the world.

"All this for a college degree? Wait until I have another big milestone. What will it be then? A cruise or a trip to an exotic island?"

She stopped talking. Though his face didn't show it, she knew he was thinking, yet again, about how he'll be able to do all of the nice things for her that he regularly declared she deserved. His money was tight and it was a something they often talked about. She told him she didn't care that he didn't have much. He barely had a place to lay his head and something like correcting that was more of a priority than him providing luxury items and expensive trips for them.

"Sumaria, one day, I'm going to be able to provide anything your heart desires. One day, I'm going to be the kind of man you deserve because you deserve the best."

"I have the best; you are the best."

"I know, baby, but you know what I mean. I can't

do for you like I want to do for you. I can't seem to get a leg up and the minute I think I'm on my way, something pulls me back down."

"What, did something happen with your music?"

Preston had been trying, along with his best friend Anthony, to make it in the music industry and so far, they didn't have any takers.

"I don't want to have that conversation right now. I want to eat and enjoy this time with you. I have a few hundred dollars left to my name and I plan to spend it all on you and our time together."

"Prez, tell me you did not spend all of your money on me like this? That's all you have left? What happened to the rest of what you were saving?"

"Do we really have to do this now?"

Sumaria wanted to let him off the hook, but he'd been trying hard to stay on the right track. She also knew the money he had left over wouldn't cover the rent he had to pay or the other bills for the small apartment he shared with Anthony. The two of them had been the best of friends since before she met him and together, they struggled on their own since age eighteen just to make ends meet while they worked night and day, when they could, on their dreams of Anthony becoming the next star, R&B singer and Preston becoming a super producer. They had the talent, but being in Meridian, they couldn't reach the people they needed to reach while also not having the resources to get out of Meridian to get to where they needed to be. Her heart hurt for him knowing how badly he wanted to succeed. Sitting down at the table after Preston pulled her chair out, she kept her eyes on him as he sat down across from her. His face told a million stories when he was trying to hide how disappointed he was in where life had taken him, trying to take care of himself since the day he turned eighteen and actually before that. She didn't want any downers between them today. They were together and that was enough for them to celebrate.

"For someone who didn't have a role model for how to treat a woman, you sure know how to do it well and with style. This is amazing and I love you for it. You know you can talk to me about anything, right? We have that kind of a relationship where you can talk to me about anything, good or bad."

"I know, but this is a happy time and I don't want to talk about my lack of funds or how hard it keeps getting to get any kind of interest in me and Anthony's projects. I'll deal with that when I get back to Meridian."

"How? How will you deal with it? Let me help," she offered.

"No."

Sumaria expected that. Her family wasn't rich, but her parents did well for themselves; her father, a college professor and her mother a nurse. They were older than most parents of a twenty-four-year-old with her mother getting pregnant and having her at forty-five while her father was forty-eight. They spoiled her where they thought it wouldn't make her a complicated person to deal with. With the money she did have or could get from them, she would help Preston in a heartbeat, but he wouldn't let her.

The few times she did help him out because the electricity in their place was being cut off or there was something he needed that would help him get closer to his dream, she gave it without a second thought, but she knew right away that until he was able to pay her back, it would eat him alive knowing he had to lean to her to help him financially. If no one else understood his predicament, she did. His life may be happening to him, but she was connected to him and so what impacted him, impacted her too.

"Prez, you never want to talk about stuff like this. I know I'm not rich, but I can help. That's what couples do."

"No, it's what I'm supposed to do for you, not you do for me. I'm not supposed to let my girl take care of me. That's not who I am. Do you know how it feels when you have to save me? It makes me feel like less of a man," he bemoaned.

"I'm not trying to do that. I love you and I want to help you get to where you want to be. My dreams aren't the only ones that matter around this table," she declared, adamantly.

"Sumaria, don't do this. Don't turn this into some kind of fight because I won't take a handout from you."

Exhaling sharply, she pulled back her feeling of being rejected, knowing where he was coming from.

"This is going to continue to come up. I know what you're going through and all I want to do is help."

When she saw his head drop down, she knew she had gone a sentence or two too far and now she wished that she could have let it go and enjoy the moment. He was trying and she was weighing it down with worry.

"You do help. You help more than you will ever know. I just hate that my life is still where it has always been. I feel like I'm in quicksand, struggling to pull myself up and out and as soon as I think I'm ready, there isn't an olive branch being extended to help me get there. I'm not speaking about you because good or bad, you are always there for me."

"Why won't you let me help? You do stuff for me all the time when I know it's a stretch. I try to do nice things for you and to help you out and you won't let me. I want to be as good to you as you are to me."

Sumaria reached her hand across the table when Preston reached out for her. So many times, they'd had this kind of conversation and he would storm out in anger over who he was versus who he wanted to be, especially for her. She was glad he wasn't doing that now.

"I don't know what it is, but I'm working on that part of me. Speaking of working on me, I wanted to save this for later, but maybe now is a better time."

"Good news?" she asked.

"I think so, but we'll see what you think."

"Okay."

"You know how Anthony did that open mic night a few months back and I'm usually there to record and upload his videos to all the social media sites? I was even sending them around to various entertainment companies and everything."

"I know. You and Anthony have been at this for years."

"Sometime after that set, the promoter of that open mic night actually posted Anthony's set to their social media pages to promote their other upcoming events like that. Last week, someone major in the entertainment industry reached out to us through the promoter and asked us to send more music."

"What? And you're just telling me about this?"

Sumaria perked up. There was good news in his life, more of a reason to celebrate this weekend besides her graduation.

"I'm sorry. I didn't know how this would turn out. I'm sharing it with you now."

She sniggered at her ability to play victim in the midst of his causes. They were so perfect for each other.

"Yes, you are. Go ahead and finish. I'm already excited because I can see excitement on your face."

"Okay, well, we got the call last week that the media mogul wants to meet with us to see us in action in person."

"Who is this person?"

"Guess. I'll just say that his wife is your favorite all-around entertainer and he has billionaire status!"

Too excited to sit still, she leaped out of her chair, rushed around the table and sat in his lap.

"No!"

"Yes!"

"*No!*" she shouted again.

"*Yes, baby.* That's exactly who it is. We have a meeting in a week. They're paying for us to fly out to Los Angeles, the entertainment capital of this country! Do you know what that will mean if we get signed? Anthony as the talent and me as the producer?"

"You're sure it's not just Anthony they want, right? Bottom line is you're the bigger star writing and producing everything."

"Anthony and I write together, though I have a lot of songs I've written myself. He's the performer and I'm the producer behind the scene where I want to be. They actually asked about the writer and if there was a producer. I told them I not only write and produce but I play all of the instruments, keyboard, drums, all that they're hearing. That's when we were both asked to fly out. Of course, we have no money for that. Any money Anthony and I have ever been able to rustle up has been to survive with a roof over our heads and to buy equipment to make our music. They're covering the flight and Anthony has a cousin who is allowing us to stay in his basement for a week while we're there."

Sumaria peppered his face with kisses as she

danced around in his lap moving her hips from side to side in sync with his body movements under her.

"I'm proud of you. I know you're going to knock this opportunity right out of the park. We now have more reasons to celebrate."

"I know. Do you know what this could mean for us? If I get signed, we can find a place in Los Angeles together and build a life there; you and me."

"That sounds amazing! Me in Los Angeles! I can see me now hobnobbing with the rich and famous because we'll be rich and famous too."

She was already picturing a life on the west coast and far away from the south. She loved her parents and all that they have done for her, but she couldn't wait to explore the world with Preston. It's all they've talked about for years.

"You can really put that interior design degree to big use out there. The sky is the limit for us."

When Preston kissed her lips, she felt the sky open up and invite them into the next step on their journey and she was ready for it. Together, they could accomplish anything.

"How will you survive with only a few dollars in your pocket? You can't go to California on a few hundred dollars for a whole week."

"Don't you worry your pretty little head about anything. I have survived not having a mother or father for years, living anywhere I could find a spot and barely having food sometimes when I was younger. I can handle a week on what I have. Anthony and I can figure it out. He's my best friend and we've always figured it out."

"What happens if this doesn't pan out? You're coming back, right?"

Sumaria didn't realize until he'd actually said the words that this opportunity could possibly take him away from her, at least temporarily. She was just about to start a new job and even if things turned out well for Preston, success wouldn't be so swift that she could pack up and move right away.

"I don't know, yeah, I guess I'll have to come back and come up with a new plan."

"I know what you want out of life and I know you can make it. I don't want you to be devastated if this doesn't work out. We may not have the lifestyle of the rich and famous in Meridian, but we'll have each other and we'll figure it out."

Sumaria not only spoke the words out loud to encourage him, she did it to encourage herself that nothing will keep them apart.

"I know we will."

"I'm happy for you. I know this is major and the best part is that I can't wait for us to plan out our life together. If that's in Meridian, we'll be okay. If it's someplace else, we'll make that work too."

"I know we will, but more than anything else, I don't want our future to be here in Meridian. I know there is a lot the south may be able to offer us, but that's really all you. You're the one with the college degrees. I barely made it out of high school. There isn't much more than the streets available for me. I want to take us away from here. If you're worried about your parents, I get that, but they'll be fine and can visit us wherever we live. If this works out, we'll be across the country."

"And if it doesn't? What will you do? I'm not trying to be a Debbie-downer, I just want us to think about both ends of the spectrum and be prepared for whatever the outcome is."

"I don't want to think about that right now. I want to celebrate your graduation and that's all I want to focus on."

"I'll keep my fingers crossed that it will all work out."

Sumaria didn't want to say more because that more sounded unsupportive in her head. She was ready for them to figure their life out where they were and with what they knew it could be without dreams so big that they couldn't figure out how to reach them. Still, now wasn't a moment to find the negative. She would be waiting for him at the airport when he returned and they would figure things out.

"With all of this celebrating we're doing, I think my hunger for food took a backseat the minute you plopped down in my lap."

Sumaria giggled when he moved his hips around to make sure she knew what he was talking about.

"I'm ready for a ride if you are. We can eat later."

Before she knew what was happening, Preston had lifted her up and headed back to the bedroom. The night was still young, but she didn't care if they stayed in bed until they had to checkout from the hotel. There was a lot to be celebrated and there was no better way to seal their love than in each other's arms.

2
One Week Later

Preston knew that despite the life he lived growing up, pretty much raising himself, he was not meant to give up. What he and Anthony hoped would happen during their trip to Los Angeles didn't pan out that way. Their meeting got cancelled again and again and then finally when they thought they were about to have the sit down to discuss next steps, they were told that a decision would take some time and, in the meantime, the executives at *Big Fella Records* wanted to see them making more of a name for themselves and the best way for them to do that would be if he and Anthony made a move to Los Angeles and really got their hustle on. The record company would send scouts out to any shows they could book around town in order to see the kind of response they get from people and to actually see them in action. They did a few meetings with some junior executives, but not the people they were promised they would get to meet and perform for.

No contract would be signed, but when the executives saw the work behind their hustle, if they were up for taking a leap in the competitive Los Angeles environment, they looked forward to having them back around the table together to discuss more possibilities. They were praised for their talent and were told that they had what it would take to make it big, but so did so many others. They wanted him and Anthony to prove what made them stand out from everyone else. In other words, it was time to really show and prove. Their success could be coming sooner rather than later if they were serious enough to go for it.

When the meeting was over and they were back at Anthony's cousin's house thinking about the next master plan, they came up with the best decision for them and that was to move to Los Angeles. Anthony's cousin, Carlos and his wife were allowing them to stay and rehearse in his basement for as long as they needed with a promise to look out for him when they finally got their come up. With a place to stay and rehearse, that was all they needed, besides a job in the meantime so that they could survive. If they got the right gigs, that may be the small income they would need to get by; handouts. With the decision to move to Los Angeles made, he knew telling Sumaria wasn't going to be easy.

After their weekend in Miami, they had talked more throughout the week and he promised her that if things didn't work out, he would return home and they would plan out their life together. She had already gotten a post-graduation job at a major finance company while she also did some work on the side doing house and apartment staging along with some work at internal department store floor designing. He loved her hustle and the fact that she was diving into the career she wanted, but he was still at stage one of working toward his goals in life and he knew that moving back to Meridian wasn't it. He only needed to get Sumaria to understand.

After Anthony left with his cousin to visit some friends, he stepped outside into the backyard of the house and sat back in a white metal rocking chair and dialed her phone. After several rings, he was about to leave a voicemail message when she answered with a low sounding hello.

"Hey, baby. How are you? I'm calling to let you know that things didn't go so well, but there is hope for something in the future."

"I'm sorry to hear that. I know you had high hopes."

Preston was surprised at the flat tone of her response. Even though his news wasn't good news, he thought that she'd be happy to hear from him.

"True, but it's not the end of the road," he said.

He started to say more, but stopped when he thought he heard something that sounded like crying. It was soft and faint, but he could hear it. It was coming from Sumaria.

"Right," she said softly.

He could hear her voice cracking and anything he wanted to share became secondary. When she didn't say more, he knew something was not right.

"What's wrong, baby? Talk to me. What's going on?" he pleaded.

"My dad. He went to the store yesterday early in the morning and didn't return. We didn't know where he was."

"What? Where is he? Do you need me to come home? I can be on the next flight home."

Preston could feel his heart racing with worry, knowing how close Sumaria was with her parents, especially her father. It was because of her father that he wanted to be a better man for her. He admired the way her father loved his wife, a strong contrast from the life he'd lived and what he saw from his mother and father.

"He's been found, but he's not well. He was found wandering around Birmingham, Alabama, a state away and without his car. I found out today from his doctor that he was diagnosed with Alzheimer's almost a year ago and he never told us. He has some other health issues as well that we didn't know about. He never told us, Prez."

"Where is he now?"

"He's here in Birmingham in the hospital. We'll be heading back to Meridian in a few days. Me and my mom are staying in a hotel and trying to figure this all out. Apparently, he went out to pick up some stuff and never did; he kept on driving. He said he couldn't remember how to get back home. The car eventually ran out of gas and he just walked away from it. He even left the keys inside of it on the side of the road. We filed a missing person's report and the car had been located before they located my dad because the car had been towed early the next morning."

"Is he going to be okay?"

"No. He has Alzheimer's. He won't get better. My mom said the day they left after my graduation and drove back home, it took a long time and my father kept getting lost though they'd taken that road many times all the years I was at school. She knew something was wrong but he's so stubborn, he would change the subject and get mad at her, so she kept the peace and didn't say anything."

"That's terrible. I'm sorry to hear this."

"It's the worst. When are you coming back? I'm sorry things didn't work out, but we can figure this out. With my jobs, I can get a place and we can move in together."

Preston sighed, knowing this wasn't the time to lay something heavy on her to add weight to what she was already going through.

"This is the deal. Anthony and I talked it over and we're going to stay out here in Los Angeles."

He waited, expecting her to blow up at him, but he had to do what he had to do.

"You're going to do what? Why would you do that? You said things didn't work out."

"I know, but they want to see more from us and then we can get another meeting with them in a few months. They want to see our social media presence ramped up and get some local gigs to really get out there and get an audience. We can do that much better from here than from Meridian."

"But, you did it from Meridian and that got you the initial sit down. You can't do that again?"

"I'm sure I could, but why would I want to do that?" he asked and then regretted the words. She spoke up before he could change his question.

"Because I'm here. What kind of life are we going to have with you in Los Angeles and me here in Meridian?"

"Baby, I'm trying to do this for us. Anthony's cousin is letting us stay with him and as long as we kick in something for the electricity, we can stay with him rent free."

"What about me?"

"You can come here with me. The jobs you have, you can find that same kind of work here. We actually talked about that too."

"That was before things didn't work out and before my father got sick. He won't recover from this or did you not hear me. I can't just leave him to my mother to care for. She wants him home and that would be a lot for her to do on her own. I have to be close to help her and you promised you would be coming back if you didn't get an offer or a contract, and you didn't. You can build your brand and social media presence from anywhere."

"Sumaria, I know and I hear you, but think of the opportunities available by being here in the middle of everything. You would love it here. The night life is amazing and we've been to some nice events and rubbed shoulders with some of today's hottest stars. We need to keep this momentum and I could lose that if I moved back to Meridian. There isn't much for me to do there. Yes, we can be together, but whatever life we'll have, that's on you and then what about me? Should I move in with you and watch you get up for work every day and pay all the bills? What kind of job would I get? I've done the fast-food thing, I worked on a city truck, I worked in a warehouse and in a few auto garages. That's pennies compared to what I could be making out here. We could get this music thing off the ground. There are people her that I could shop my songs to. This is where everything is happening."

"You promised, Prez. You promised and now I'll be here alone dealing with this. I guess you've made your choice."

"Wait, what? There is no choice here. I'm still choosing us and I want you to choose us too."

"No, you're asking me to choose you over my parents and to move and live who knows where in hopes that your career will take off. Maybe that's not for you. Did you ever think of that?"

Preston's heart sank at her disparaging tone knowing she was responding out of anger and stress over what was happening with her father and he would give her space to do that.

"I know you're hurting right now and I understand. Your father is sick and it's hard on you and from what I hear, it will get harder. What do you really want me to do?"

"I want you to come back here and be with me."

"Baby, I can do that for a few weeks, but not permanently. You know what my music means to me."

"I need you to move back here for good, not just for a few weeks."

"And do what while I'm there?" he questioned.

"Be with me. I just said that. What you went out there to do didn't work out and you said you would come back and now you're telling me either I go be with you or you'll stay out there without me. In essence, you're leaving me."

"I'm not doing that. I would never do that. I'm still trying to make a life for us here."

"Doesn't sound like you're doing it there either. I have to go. Don't come back for a visit if you're not going to stay. Sounds like your mind is made up and I wish you well. After all these years, you're finally showing me that you would choose your career or one you don't have yet over our love. Thanks a lot for breaking me down further than where I'm finding myself these days. I can't take much more of anything. You go and have your life. I'll be fine here. Bye, Preston."

He knew things were bad when she called him Preston instead of Prez. She never did that. When he went to speak up, she had hung up on him. When he tried to dial her back, she wouldn't answer. Seven or eight times, he tried to reach her, leaving her a voicemail each time. His last one was left with the last bit of strength he had.

"Baby, it's me again. I wish you would pick up, but I understand. You're under a lot of pressure right now. I'll give you a few days and call you back. I'm not leaving you – I'm finding a future for us. I wish you would talk to me and let's work this out. Please call me back. I love you, Sumaria. Please call me back."

He hung up and waited.

3
Three Years Later

Preston walked into the back of the church and looked at the many unfamiliar faces collectively mourning a loss. It's been three years since he last stepped foot in Meridian, Mississippi and though a lot has changed, most of the neighborhoods he drove through on his way to the funeral hadn't changed. If it hadn't been for Anthony who had recently returned to Meridian to connect with a woman from his past, he never would have known that Sumaria's mother had died or that her funeral was today. Luckily, he was able to get a flight from Los Angeles earlier in the morning and arrived as people were still walking around to greet the family.

As floods of people walked by him, he didn't feel like now was the time to make his presence known to Sumaria, so he found a seat and sat down. He had no problem waiting. He'd waited three long years to come back, finally as the man he always wanted to be for her.

She was there with him through it all and though it hurt him to leave her and not return to Meridian, he had to do what he needed to do in order to look her in the eyes as the man who could hold his head up with strong shoulders and who could love and take care of her. What he didn't know was that in the last three years that he'd been gone, she'd lost both her father and her mother; her father to Alzheimer's two years ago and her mother, just recently, to a heart attack.

The homegoing service was beginning and when people all over the church began to sit, he could see Sumaria in the seat on the aisle of the front row. Next to her, he saw her best friend, Tara, who he already knew would be by her side. They had been the best of friends through the years. The row was filled with a few other faces he remembered seeing at holiday gatherings at Sumaria's house over the years, but he didn't remember any names.

Throughout the crowd, a few people who remembered him from years ago waved and others, including the woman who sat next to him recognized him from the career he now had in the music industry and even at a funeral, whispered to him to try and get his autograph. He ignored them and pointed to the preacher in the pulpit, letting them know that they should be paying attention to the service and not to him. The last thing he wanted to do was to be a distraction which is why he didn't bring his usual security along with him. This was a personal trip and he wanted to handle it as lowkey as he could.

When his eyes again traveled to Sumaria, he was overwhelmed by her beauty just as he always had been since the moment he met her. She was a cheerleader and at that time, the girlfriend of the star quarterback. He first spotted her at a pep rally and watched her throughout the pre-game activities and during the game when he should have been focused on the game on the field. With Sumaria in her short green and white skirt and pure, bright white sneakers with beauty beyond belief, he knew he had to meet her. Her hair was long and flowed down her back, moving around likes waves on the ocean as her head moved. Her smile was perfect and everything about her stood out. The next day at school, he searched her out and even got into a bit of a scuffle with her then boyfriend who caught him eyeing her during lunch.

After school, he saw her getting on a bus and raced to catch her. Before he got far, he was thrown off the bus as he tried to climb the stairs after being told he was not scheduled to be on that bus. He wasn't scheduled to be on any bus. He'd been riding a bike back and forth to school on the days when he would actually show up. He could have been on the bus, but back then, he was embarrassed with how he looked. He didn't want to be the butt of people's jokes on the bus, so he avoided it.

As the bus drove by him, he searched out her face. When she saw him, he winked hoping she would smile or even wave. Instead, she whipped her head around and ignored him as if he were a leper. He knew he would have another chance and that chance came a few days later.

He'd been in class when he saw her walk by in the hallway outside. He slipped out of class, to the dismay and disapproval of his teacher. Once in the hallway, he caught up with her and he tried talking as if he really had a chance. He still remembered that day how dirty his pants and shirt were as he tried to hide the spots from her view. He knew who her friends were and they often looked down on him because of the unkept way he would often dress. It was no one's business that he had to try and wash his clothes by hand when his mother bought drugs with the little money they had and left none for getting laundry done. He made the best of his situation and still, he wanted Sumaria. She may shoot him down, but maybe not.

He asked her for her name and she turned around so fast as they walked that he ended up walking right into her. As the preacher spoke from the pulpit as the funeral proceeded, he thought back to how that conversation went on that first day of finally drawing her attention.

"Sorry, I didn't mean to bump into you. I was trying to get your name," he said.

"Why do you need my name?" she asked him.

"What?"

"Why do you need my name, especially since I

know that you already know my name? You've been asking people about me and my boyfriend doesn't like it."

"Yeah, I know and that fist fight we had in the cafeteria proved that, but that didn't mean I wouldn't still try to get to know you. It's not a crime to talk to someone else even when you have a boyfriend or should I say an ex-boyfriend."

"Cameron is not my ex-boyfriend."

"He will be after this conversation, Sumaria."

"I thought you didn't know my name."

"Okay, I lied. I just wanted a reason to talk to you. Can we talk?"

"We are talking."

"Can I take you out sometime?"

"I have a boyfriend."

"You mentioned that, but that wasn't an answer to my question."

"If you had a girlfriend would you want another guy to be asking her out?"

"No and if I had a girlfriend, I would treat her so good that she wouldn't even consider it."

"I'm not considering it."

"Sure you are because I'm a great person. I'm handsome and I would treat you like a queen."

"Really? How would you do that and don't say by buying me stuff because my father already buys me whatever I want. Any guy interested in me has to come better than that."

"Oh, so you are considering it or you would have said no and walked away. Okay, I got you. I'm not talking about material stuff. I'll reserve that for after we get married one day."

"Married? You go from asking my name, to asking me out, to assuming we'll get married one day?"

"I sure did. That's how confident I am that once you get to know me, you'll like me. Like I was saying, I'm not talking about stuff, but I can say this and if you want to know more, you'll have to go out with me. I'm not one to gossip but your boy is playing you and you should check him on that and that girl on your squad with the red streaks in her hair. I would never do you like that, but I'll let you seek and find the truth for yourself. My girlfriend would never have to worry about me hitting up another girl because she would know if I'm about her. I want to be all about you. All I'm asking is for a date to get a burger or something. I mean, I'm not rich and I barely have enough money to feed myself most days, but I have twenty dollars and I want to spend it all on you."

"And what would you eat?"

"I'd starve because my priority is making sure you're happy and can eat what you want first. A true boyfriend seeks out your needs before his own, even if he has to starve."

That was the moment he'd won her over. A week later, he was talking to a group of friends near his locker and she walked right up to him and said that he could take her out and that it would take the entire twenty dollars. That was the happiest day of his life and what he didn't tell her was that he didn't really have twenty dollars, but he knew he would get it. He tried borrowing it from a few friends, but they were just as broke as he was. He never told her that he lifted a twenty from his mother's wallet while she slept off her latest high that Saturday afternoon and when they met for burgers, he spent every penny on her. She told him how she checked her boyfriend about the girl on her cheerleader squad that she heard he was also seeing and being who he was, Cameron the football quarterback and the most popular guy at the school, he didn't deny it and told her that she should be lucky that he chose her. She broke up with him and didn't look back.

He and Sumaria were inseparable from that day forward, until he left Meridian to chase a dollar and a dream and though it took him a couple of years to get where he knew he could be, he did and he was coming back to Meridian to claim his love; to get back his heart. He came back for Sumaria not knowing what her life was like now.

He did find out that she no longer lived in Meridian, but that was all he knew. He didn't even know if she'd gotten married, but from the looks of what he could see with her sitting alone with Tara, he assumed if she had a boyfriend or husband, he'd be next to her consoling her in her time of need.

His heart still ached for the woman he didn't come back to three years ago. After trying to reach her to reason with her, they had spoken a handful of times and then one day, her cell phone number was changed and he never heard from her again. He thought they were beginning to work things out but her pleas for him to come back and his rejection to do so had begun to tire her out and she soon had enough.

When they had spoken, none of the conversations went well. She accused him of abandoning her, yet he saw it as finally having a chance to make something of himself; to turn into someone worthy of her. He couldn't do that in Meridian and it took everything in him to finally let her go when she told him she was done and couldn't wait for him to find himself when all he needed was their love. To her, she believed a mediocre life could sustain them and he wanted more, not just for him, but for them together.

He'd waited long enough to come back for her. He respected her need to look after her parents and knew that nothing he could say could pull her away and he didn't want to do that. She needed to be where she was and he needed to be where he was, making something presentable of himself.

For three long years, he worked and he waited. He built up his life and his career and he waited. There was no doubt she knew how his career had finally taken off a year after he left Meridian. His come-up was major news when he and Anthony got the chance to release their first three songs and all three were major hits, big money makers and the contract they each eventually signed skyrocketed their careers. Since then, especially in the last year, he had written mega hits for the country's top artist and made more money than he could have dreamed of. From that, he and Anthony were using their newfound fame and fortune to start their own label with a new artist that every major was trying to land, but in the end, he and Anthony signed him and the rest, as they say, is history. He was on his way to the top and the one empty spot in his life was a woman. Not just any woman; only Sumaria. Being of the most recognizable producers in the industry meant nothing if he couldn't get Sumaria back. He did it all for her.

He thought about returning many times to claim their love, but he didn't think she was ready. Once, about a year ago, he was a few hours outside of Meridian and decided to hop in a rental car and just drive and found himself sitting outside of the house her parents had lived in. He wasn't sure he'd be welcomed, but he'd finally gotten the nerve and was about to walk up the seven steps to the door when a man walked out and greeted him. He'd never seen the man before. He appeared to be around fifty, pudgy around the middle and smoking a nasty smelling pipe. When he told the man who he was looking for, the man told him that his son and daughter-in-law were renting the house from a management company and he didn't know anything about the owners or where they were.

He felt defeated that day. After getting the nerve to see Sumaria, he found she wasn't there and neither was her mother and father. He got in his car and drove out of Meridian knowing that he had no reason to return. He tried looking he up since she had a rare name, but that didn't pan out. She was one of those people who made sure her name and contact information were not readily available on the internet through various online telephone directories. His number hadn't changed and he was specific about that. If she ever wanted to reach out to him again, he wanted to be sure she could call the last number she had for him. To his disappointment, she never did. When she told him she was done, she clearly meant it.

Seeing her now, he knew they weren't done or over. Just like in high school when she had a boyfriend and he told her that she would be his, he meant it then and he knew it now. Unless she was engaged or married to someone else, he was coming for her.

When she turned her head to the side, his heart began a rapid beating. The organ in his chest still had nothing but love for her and seeing her, the love he held for her was in the heart that she carried around with her that belonged to him, though she no longer cared or was even aware of. How he would approach her, he didn't know, but he'd come this far and now wasn't the time to turn back. He kept his eyes on her knowing only an hour or so is what continued to keep them apart, but that would soon end and it was either do, or it was die alone without her because there wasn't another woman that could hold a torch to the love he had for her; none.

~~

Sumaria stood for a few extra moments alone at her mother's final resting place, right with her father, where her mother longed to be.

After losing her father, her mother had never recovered from her broken heart. Even her doctor mentioned that she couldn't find a medical reason of why her mother suddenly died in her sleep in their home in Atlanta. That was where she'd moved and made a home when an opportunity she couldn't pass up came her way and she was able to move her parents with her to a nice house in an Atlanta suburb. She'd made a nice home for them until her father was no longer manageable at home. She found a nice place not far from where they lived where her mother could visit him every day. After turning over their house in Meridian to a management company to manage and rent out, she packed up their lives and to Atlanta they went.

When her father died, she had his body brought back to Meridian for his final burial. They had once told her that no matter where they were in the world, when they died, they wanted to be buried in their hometown in the same cemetery with other family members. Shockingly, one morning she went into her mother's room to wake her for breakfast and found her still in bed. She thought it odd that her mother didn't stir when she called out to her. Walking around the bed, she found her mother still under the covers with her eyes wide open and she was gone. For six months, day in and day out, her mother mourned the husband she'd met as a teenager and struggled to get through life without him. Sumaria had heard of that type of thing happening. Bringing her mother back to Meridian to be buried with the only man she loved was her duty and so back to Meridian she again came. Though the city held some good memories for her, it wasn't a place of pure joy and happiness that had her longing to return. There were good memories but there were also not so good memories. With her parents now gone, she could finally put Meridian behind her and actually move on with her life. She had a lot to live and thrive for and the time to do so was now.

"I miss you mommy and daddy. We're going to be fine and thank you for a lifetime of love that I'll always carry with me. Take your rest and I'll see you again one day in glory. I have to leave now, but I want to say these words from your favorite song by Myrna Summers', Uncloudy Day '*Oh they tell me of a home, far beyond the sky; Oh they tell me of a home, so far away; Yes, they tell me of a home, where no storm clouds arise; Oh they tell me, yes they tell me of an uncloudy day.*' I'll see you there one day and we'll hug and talk about how we've missed each other. Until then, keep building our home in glory. I know it's beautiful just as you are. I love you and I promise that I will live the greatest life possible."

Blowing her last kiss to her mother's casket, she turned and walked to where the last limousine waited for her. On this hot June day in her black short sleeved dress and her black hat, one of her mother's favorites that she wore to church, she made her way. Out of the corner of her eye, she saw someone approaching her. She assumed, with the exception of the men who would see to her mother, that she was alone after sending Tara and the few other close family members back to the car to wait for her. As she got closer to the person approaching, though the sun was shining bright, she could see the outline of a man. As he walked toward her and she stood still to get a better look at him, she removed her dark shades and tried to block the sun with her hand. When she did, she couldn't believe who was now standing in front of her. Could it be? There was no way she wouldn't know who he was. Just as she mourned her parents, she had mourned the loss of his love three years ago and here he was coming up to her at the cemetery.

"Hello, Sumaria."

That voice. It's deepness. It's affection. It's loving tone. She remembered it. The way it had made her body quiver at the mere sound if it so many times. It was engrained, deep-rooted in her brain. Standing in front of her like a vision out of a men's magazine stood the man she had once loved more than anyone else in the world; the one man who had destroyed her for any other man.

"Preston."

She wanted to say more, but didn't know what she could say. What she wanted to do was run. Her life of the past three years flashed and she needed to keep it far away from him. He couldn't be here with her right now. This wasn't a good time for a lot of reasons. The greatest one was waiting for her in the limousine. She had to go; now.

"How are you? I'm sorry about your mother and your father. I didn't know that he passed away and I just heard about your mother."

"You came to Meridian for the funeral?" she asked.

"I did. That and I came to talk to you."

"After three years? About what? Now is not a good time, Preston."

"Preston? You used to call me Prez."

"I used to have a reason to call you that," she retorted.

"I know and I'm sorry. I know this is the worst time, but if I can leave you with my number, maybe we can go for coffee or something. Maybe burgers?"

He was trying to make the conversation lighter and she knew the meaning was to send her thoughts back to when they met and he asked her out on their first date and they went for burgers. Well, they weren't teenagers anymore and she didn't want to eat a burger with him or drink coffee with him. She wanted him to leave and let her get back to her life. She was still trying to work him out of her system even after all of this time and then he shows up and asks her to coffee and old feelings overpower her senses. There was no way he still held this kind of power over her; over her heart, but he did. She won't admit, though.

"No coffee or burgers or anything else. I can't."

Trying to walk around him, she quickened her steps knowing her escape was ahead of her and all she had to do was get to the car and get out of there and away from. She had nothing to say.

"Sumaria, please? I just want to talk."

She stopped when she reached the car and turned back to him.

"There is nothing to talk about; not now, not ever. Go back to your life and let me get back to mine."

"Listen, I know I hurt you, but I'm hoping you could give me a few minutes of your time and attention. Is that asking too much after the history we have together?"

Now she was angry. How dare he come back after leaving her and acting as if she owed him anything.

"That history didn't persuade you to choose me back then and I don't choose to give you my time now. Go back home Preston. There is nothing here for you."

She saw him open his mouth to speak again and when she opened the car door, she watched his shoulders slump as he turned and began walking away.

Just then, as if somewhere, someone was intervening to make her confront her past, there was a screech from inside the car and before she knew it, a voice cried out which not only stopped her from getting in, but stopped Preston from moving.

"Mommy, mommy!"

No, she screamed in her head. Then she heard it again, this time, it was louder.

"Mommy, mommy!"

There was no way she was going to be able to avoid the pleas of a child, but she couldn't and didn't move. Her feet were glued as Preston turned all the way around and walked closer to her just as Aiden climbed from the second row of the limousine where he should have been sleeping and into the front seat where he reached out for her, screaming her name louder and louder, crying until she finally reached for him and cradled him in her arms until he quieted. She now had no escape. Preston moved closer to her and saw her rocking her son as he quieted and just like that, she knew that he knew. She could see the wheels turning in his head as he tried to play out in his mind how old the child she was holding was. He could assume she had a child with someone else, but something in his face told her that he wasn't thinking that. He was thinking something else entirely. He was thinking what she knew to be true.

"Who...who is that?" Preston stuttered out.

"Mommy, I'm hungry."

"Mommy? He's calling you mommy?" he asked.

As Aiden played with pressing his fingers into her cheeks as he liked to do, she couldn't avoid the inevitable and knew how close she had been to going back to her life in Atlanta. She had been so close.

"Go back to Aunt Tara and I promise to get you something to eat. Tara, strap him in. I thought he was asleep."

"Sumaria? Who is that? How old is he and before you answer, let me just say that I got a good look at him and if I had one of my baby pictures with me, the face I see on him would be the same face in the picture. How old is he?" he pressed her.

"Preston, let it go. It's been a lot of time and we both have our lives. Let me go," she said and tried to turn to get in the car.

"Sumaria, when I tell you that I'm not leaving Meridian until we talk, I mean it. If that's my son, you better tell me right now. Again, who is he?"

She reminded herself that there was no escape and the secret she'd been keeping from him for three years was now out in the open and he was right, Aiden looked just like him; just like his daddy.

"His name is Aiden and he's my son; our son."

She stood still and waited for his response but what she got was him taking a few steps back while covering his mouth, clearly shocked at the revelation. His eyes widened and he looked from her to the car and then back over at her.

"What?"

"Look, you can go back to your life and Aiden will be fine. You don't have any obligation."

"What? You were pregnant? When and why didn't you tell me?"

"Not here. I can't do this here."

"Oh, I don't care what you think you can and cannot do. You just told me I have a son who is what? How old?"

"He's two and a half."

"You were pregnant when I left and you never told me? You didn't tell me you were pregnant. How could you do that to me? How could you? We talked weeks after I left. Weeks, Sumaria."

Preston wasn't angry as much as she saw the hurt on his face and in his eyes. When he turned and headed away from her, she didn't know if she wanted to run after him or let him go. As she struggled with what to do, she was surprised to see him turn back toward her, reach into his pocket and go through is wallet, taking out a card and handing it to her.

"What's this?" she asked turning it over and reading it.

"It's my number which has not changed in three years. You need to call me and we need to talk and before you try to think you're keeping me from my son, think again."

Before she could respond, Preston walked away faster than she would be able to catch him. This time he was angry. He spoke to her through clinched teeth and walked away. Not knowing what else to do, she sat in the front seat of the limo and asked the driver to get her back to her hotel. She didn't look back for Preston and hoped that his anger was temporary and that he would see that he didn't need to reach back in his past. He could get back on a plane and go back to his life and leave her to hers. That's what she was hoping he would do. Her plan wasn't to wait around to see what he would do. She was getting out of Meridian immediately.

4

Two days and still nothing; nothing at all. No word, no smoke signal, not even a pigeon messenger. Preston was now in his second day in Meridian and he had not heard from Sumaria, kicking himself for walking away from her knowing he should have made her explain how she could keep the fact that he had a son away from him. Not only were his days stressful, but the night before, he hadn't gotten any sleep at all and the lack of sleep didn't take his impatient energy away. He had been pretty much sitting on his phone waiting for her to call and yet, he got nothing. He now knew that he should have gotten her number instead of just thrusting his number at her and expecting her to call. If she hadn't done so all this time, why did he expect she would now? He didn't and that pissed him off even more.

What he finally came to realize is that she wasn't going to call. He wasn't going to get the chance to talk to her or see his son. She had a lot of explaining to do and he wasn't going to let her off easy. Still in all of his anger, his love for her didn't lessen. He was madder than he'd ever been in his life over not knowing about Aiden, but still, he loved her as much as he always had and his reason for returning to Meridian did not change. He was still in town for her and now that also included his son. He had a son! Saying the words had his mind all over the place. His first thought was how could she keep Aiden from him? She knew the kind of life he had and how he always said he would not be the kind of father he, himself had. When his phone rang, he leaped for it where it had fallen between the chair cushions. Seeing Anthony's face on the screen, it wasn't Sumaria and that pained him.

"Bro, what's going on!" Anthony hollered at him.

Preston plopped down on the sofa, shirtless and clad only in a pair of black sweat pants.

"Where do I begin."

"Did you see her? Speak to her? I bet she's still as gorgeous as she was before. Did the two of you play kissy face?" Anthony joked.

"No. My son was too busy poking her cheeks," he tossed out and waited.

"Who? What son? Fool, what are you talking about? You don't have a son. You went to Meridian for a funeral and to reclaim your woman. What son? Are you drunk?"

"Not drunk enough, but after I run to the store, I

will definitely get there before the night is over."

"Then what?"

"There's so much to tell you, but right now, I don't have all the answers. Sumaria was pregnant when you and I left for L.A. three years ago and I didn't know it. She never told me, had my son and kept him from me. She never said a word. My number hasn't changed. You know I kept it for that reason because I wanted her to always be able to reach me if she wanted to. Just because she didn't want to didn't mean she shouldn't have told me she was pregnant."

"What! Wow, man. That is crazy. How old is he and what's his name? Are you getting to know him? Take his picture and send it to me."

"That's the problem. Not only do I not have a picture to send you but I haven't seen him – only a glimpse at the cemetery. I could tell she was trying to rush me off but then this little boy called her mommy and she couldn't get away fast enough. She would have been happy if an earthquake or a flood had happened to take the focus off the fact that she was about to play escape artist with my son a few feet away from me. I mean, I was right there and she would have let me leave and never said a word. If he hadn't called for her, I would still be in the dark."

"What did she say? How did she explain herself?"

"She didn't. Stupid me, I gave her my number and told her we needed to talk. In the middle of a cemetery was not the place to talk."

"She didn't call, huh?"

"Not even a peep; nothing; nada."

"Do you know where she lives? Is she still in Meridian somewhere?"

"I don't know and at this point, I don't know what to do. I'll tell you this, she's not keeping me from my son. I don't care where she lives. I'm not leaving here until I see her and see my son."

"I have a concert in Vegas tonight and tomorrow. I assume you're not going to make it?" Anthony asked.

Preston forgot all about his life and now with this new twist, he couldn't go back to it yet.

"I'm going to miss that. Luckily, I have some free time before meeting about some songs I've been asked to collaborate on for an upcoming movie. I'm going to hang around and try to connect with Sumaria. I know she believes I'm pissed at her, which I am, but not like she thinks I am. I love her too much to be angry at her to the point that I can't come back from it. I have a son and she didn't tell me. She went on with her life and left me hanging. I have a son. Can you believe that?"

"I can't, but hearing you say it is making it quite real. I can't wait to meet a little version of you. From what you saw of him, does he look like you?"

"He is my twin. How can she look in his face day in and day out and not think about me? He is me as a little boy. I can't leave here without my son. I can't just walk away."

"I know where you're going with this and I

understand; I get it. I know what a real bastard your father was and the way your mother did you was horrible, tossing you out on your eighteenth birthday when she found out she would no longer get any money or food benefits anymore since you were an adult."

Preston hated thinking about those days, but he also appreciated them because it was those days that made him push so hard to make something of himself. He was an only child, never knew any of his family on either side and had a father who wished he hadn't been born.

"Those days were rough. There were times when I didn't know if I would have a roof over my head when the sun went down. I slept on concrete floors with no blanket, a few times, I slept in alleys behind a dumpster just to get out of the rain. If it wasn't for you and Sumaria, I wouldn't be here today. Did I ever tell you that when I was in high school, not long after I met her, my mother would kick me out at least once a week because she expected me to be out on the streets selling drugs to provide for her. I had no money, no phone, no nothing. I would go to school just to be able to eat. It was me and that bike. When she found out, she would let me come by her house after her parents had gone to sleep and I would shower and she would fix me sandwiches and give me bags of other food to eat that didn't need to be cooked like peanut butter and jelly with bread and crackers. She would even bring me food to school and we would find a corner and she'd sneak it to me so that no one would know. When she could get away with it, she would let me sleep on her floor next to her bed, tossing me a blanket and pillow. There was no sex or not even much talking and I was thankful for that. She did so much for me and all I ever wanted to do was have the kind of life where I could give her the world. She never understood me leaving Meridian, but I couldn't come back. There was nothing that I could do in life here to make a life for us. Now that I can and I came back to see if there was any love left between us, I find that she's the world's best secret keeper. She was pregnant and had my baby and I didn't know. If she doesn't call me, I don't know how to reach her. I tried before and got nowhere and that was about two years ago."

"What are you going to do?"

"I don't know. I have to find her. I can't go back to L.A. as if I didn't just find out I have a whole son who looks just like me. My father was the worst kind of man. He would see me as a kid and would purposely walk on the other side of the street to avoid talking to me. He cursed me, threw his middle finger up at me and one time, I was sitting on the steps of the apartment I lived in with my mother and he walked up and banged me in my face. I had a black eye for days. He never said a word; just walked up, hit me and walked away. Left me sitting there crying. I was seven or eight years old. Do you know what my mother said?" he asked.

"I'm almost afraid to ask about that witch that was

your mother. I'm not expecting much, so hit me with it," Anthony exclaimed.

"Nothing. She didn't say anything. I told her what happened and she said that I should remember to bob and weave the next time."

"Your mom was cold, dude; cold as friggin' ice!"

"As I got older, I would see him around and still, he acted like I was a stranger to him. Just before he was found dead from an overdose, I saw him one day and he walked right up to me. I was about seventeen and I thought that he wanted to talk and finally get to know me and I was ready to embrace him. Instead, he asked me for money and when I didn't have it to give to him, he said that he knew I was nothing and not worth a dime anyway. He died leaving those as the last words he said to me."

"Yeah, I remember how you felt after that. I found you hitting your fists against a wall and Sumaria bandaged your bloody knuckles and you got over that and realized he wasn't worth the heartache you suffered because of a man who didn't want to be your father."

"True and that's why I can't just walk away from Aiden. I don't even know him, but he's my son and now that I do know about him, I don't want another day of his life to go forth without him knowing me and hearing my voice, knowing I'm his daddy. Sumaria took that away from me until now, but not anymore. I will see my son."

"What about that girl she was best friends with? Tara? Where is she?"

"I saw her at the funeral, but I didn't get a chance to talk to her."

"If I can do anything to help, I'm a phone call away. If you need me in Meridian, all you have to do is speak it and I'm on the first thing smoking out of the west coast. You hear me?"

"I got you and I appreciate it. I'm going to think about my next step. I don't even know if Sumaria is still in Meridian. For all I know, she hightailed it out of here and back to her life. She doesn't know that I don't care if she's living on the moon these days, I'd steal a shuttle and fly to her and my son. I'll figure it out. Good luck with the concert and don't worry about me. I'll be fine. I'll reach out either tomorrow or the next day and give you an update."

"Alright. I'm keeping two fingers in the air for you and I know you'll get to see your son soon. Holla!" Anthony shouted and then call ended.

Wishing he did have a drink because a nice, stiff one would help in a major way, he thought about all of the ways he could intrude in Sumaria's life and find her and his son, but he didn't want to go about it that way. He would lose her for sure. He needed an ally and he needed a plan.

He laid his head back on the soft, plush cushion of the sofa and tried to wrap his head around the fact that he had a son and just as fast as he'd found out about him, he was gone and to where, he didn't know but he would find out.

~~

"You're really doing this? You're going to leave Meridian like a thief in the night and take that man's son with you without so much as a few words to him? How can you do that?" Tara asked.

Sumaria rushed around the hotel room, gathering up what she could as fast as she could. She could hear her own ragged breaths and it was that sound that made her aware of how desperate she was the get back to her life. Never in a million years did she think she'd run into Preston again. She had no qualms about returning to Meridian to bury her mother just as she did with her father, but considering how much he hated the city, nothing could have prepared her to come face to face with the man her heart never forgot about, her body still yearned for and her eyes still found delight in when she set them on his handsome face.

"I can't with you right now, especially if you're not going to be supportive. I have to leave. He knows and now what am I supposed to do? He's going to want an explanation of why I kept Aiden from him and I don't have one. Outside of being bitter and angry when he didn't come back for me, I don't have another story that doesn't make me sound like a horrible person. I kept a man from his son. I kept my son from his father and now that our two worlds have crossed again, I don't know what else to do other than to buy myself some time. The only way to do that is to go home, back to familiar territory and figure out how I'm going to deal with this."

"Don't do this. Though you've been in Atlanta over two years, you were still running and you still are. Stop running from your heart; from Preston who doesn't deserve to catch a glimpse of his son and then nothing. You know I'm on your side, right or wrong, I'm on your side, but know that he's not going away."

Sumaria huffed, slowed down and sat on the edge of the bed and watched her best friend as she rocked a cranky Aiden back to sleep.

"I'm not ready. I need a little time. Did you see him? Did you see how good he looked?"

Sumaria tried with all of her might to remove the image of Preston standing before her looking like some model in a men's magazine. Preston was always handsome, but seeing him dressed up in a sharp black suit with a crisp black shirt and a diamond in one ear, she never imagined he'd be that sexy dressed up. When they were involved, he never had the kind of money or even a reason to spend money on that kind of clothing. Secretly following his career, she knew that he could afford that and so much more.

"You better get ready. You know him better than anyone and you know he's not going to stop until he talks to you. I'm surprised he hasn't already shown up here, but then again, since your uncle secured everyone's rooms, he wouldn't be able to find you by using your name. And damn, he looked good. Did he always look that good? I see why the women are all over the internet throwing themselves at him. Have you seen the bootie pictures and cleavage trying to entice him on social media? I bet his inbox be blowing up!" Tara yelled.

Sumaria tried not to let her face show that on just the idea of that, she was jealous. Of course, she'd seen his social media pages and kept up with him in the media. Her reason for not having social media under her name was so that he wouldn't find her and find out about Aiden.

"You're not helping!" she yelled and when Aiden stirred, she quieted quickly. She wasn't planning on letting him get a nap before their flight back to Atlanta, hoping he would sleep on the plane, but he was cranky and in dire need of rest. Aiden didn't sleep well in foreign places which had them both up through the night.

"Okay, I'm sorry. What do you need from me?" Tara asked.

"The house. Though the house is rented, we didn't rent the garage with it. There are a lot of my parents' things still in the garage. I have a moving company coming tomorrow to box up everything to then ship it all to me in Atlanta. Can you meet them and make sure everything is packed? Your flight to Atlanta is still in three days like my original plan. I have to leave. I need to get out of Meridian. You know how much I hate this place anyway. I lost everything here."

"Everything? You lost everything? I get it that you would feel that way, but it's not true. You're only looking at the bad, but think of this – you lost Preston, you lost your parents, but you made Aiden here and this little boy is not only your world, but he's my world too. I'm his godmother and he brings me joy. He's such a good boy, a happy boy and I know how much you love him, covet him even because you think you need to protect him from the life you feel was snatched away from you; a life of love and happiness. You blame Preston for that and though I think he was dead wrong for leaving you and choosing his career over my best friend, but I understand why he did. You have to give him that. You saw first-hand what his life was like. I saw it too."

"Did you see the hurt in his eyes? He's never looked at me that way. I've always been able to see love in his eyes, but earlier today, he was furious, maybe even filled with instant hatred. I set him free. I let him go so that he didn't feel obligated to me when I realized he didn't choose me first. Selfish of me, I know, but that's where I was. I just wanted Preston and then when I found out I was pregnant, I picked up the phone to call him so many times, but all I could think about was if the then chose me because I was pregnant, it wouldn't be for the right reason. I needed him to want me and he didn't."

Sumaria began to cry and didn't care that her ugly

cry face was showing. She was scared of what was next now that Preston knew she carried a secret.

"Don't do this to yourself. You know as well as I do that Preston has always loved you. Yeah, it sucked that he left for a temporary trip and decided to make it permanent without thinking about what it would do to you. I hated on him just like you did because that's what best friends do. I saw his face when he saw Aiden and then when you admitted Aiden was his son. When he walked away, I felt for him."

"I should have gone after him. So much in his life has been taken away. His mother kicked him out and didn't want him around anymore. His father never wanted him and when he did see him, he acted like Preston wasn't his son. He had no one and nothing and there were times I thought he would give up on himself. He now knows that I took the first two and half years of his son's life from him and I saw the look. I wish I was strong enough to come face to face with him again, but I'm not and I need your help. Can you handle the move of the garage stuff for me? I know I'm asking a lot, but I need a little more time to take in how to explain myself, not that there is a good explanation."

"Yes, I'll help. I'll need something to do being back in Meridian for a few more days. I promised my mother I'd have a spa day with her tomorrow and I'm going to spend some time with my brother and his family while I'm here. The event back in Atlanta is being handled by the best event planner in that city, so I'm not worried about that and I'll be back before your big day. I've got you covered here."

Sumaria stood, walked over and hugged Tara and Aiden together. Running her fingers through his short, curly hair, she smiled when he yawned and smiled in his sleep. He was his father's twin. She now had to figure out how to deal with the possibility that her life was changing and Preston was back in it, even if it was because they had a son. She may be running back to Atlanta to avoid him, but knowing how determined Preston was, she was only getting a little extra time. He was going to come for his son and she needed to be ready.

"This is why Aiden loves you so much, sometimes more than me, I think."

"That's because I give him good snacks when you're not looking."

"It's also because you have been by my side since we were kids and now when my life is about to get complicated, I know I can count on you."

Sumaria was about to hug Tara again, but halted when her smiled turned upside down.

"You're forgetting one thing or should I say, one person," Tara said.

Sumaria watched Tara's movements as she stood, moved slowly to place a sleeping Aiden on the bed, between the thick pillows on the bed too keep him from rolling off onto the floor.

"Don't go there and do you know why? It's because

there's nothing there."

"Oh, there's something there. He just hasn't made his move yet. Now that Preston has reappeared and I can tell from the way you're acting that the feelings you had for him are just as deep as they were three years ago, what happens when you get back to Atlanta? How will you handle that complication?" Tara asked.

"There's nothing there," Sumaria said again, more this time for herself than to respond to Tara.

"Right. I'm going to my room to make some calls since I left my phone there. Think about what I just asked. This additional complication is real whether you want to believe it or not. Before coming here, you were ready to entertain it. I think Preston changed all that, even if you don't want to admit it to me. Admit it to yourself as you're running away like a thief in the night. What are you running toward? I have the answer – an even bigger issue. I won't speak it out loud. I'll let you do that when I'm gone."

Sumaria watched Tara disappear out of the door of her hotel room and as it slammed shut, she turned and exhaled loudly, doing what Tara knew she would do. She spoke it out loud; *Hakeem.*

5

Preston watched from the rental car as Tara spoke with several men who moved boxes and other items from the garage at Sumaria's parents' house to a moving truck. He was glad that Anthony still had several contacts in Meridian who didn't have any information on Sumaria, but had seen Tara in front of the house and as soon as he got word, he hopped in his rental car and headed straight over to the house that held many memories for him; the only house he'd ever been in where the memories were good.

Sumaria had lived in that house with the short grass area in front, but a backyard larger than most school football fields. He looked over at the brick driveway that led back to a detached two-car garage, a place where Sumaria would often sneak him back to so that he could have a safe place to sleep at night when he would otherwise be living on the street. He smiled at the remembrance of nights when her parents went to be early and he would climb up the brick posters that held up the roof over the back deck. She would open her bedroom window and once inside, especially in the winter months during his senior year of high school, he would find a warm corner on her pink carpeted floor and covered up in the many blankets and pillow she'd toss his way, he would get the best sleep. Early in the morning, Sumaria would set her clock and he'd climb back out of the same window. Those were the days of his childhood that he remembered the most. The bad memories were there, but it was the days of spending time with Sumaria and her family that he loved the most. Her parents could have looked down on him and told her that she should aim higher when it came to the man she wanted to spend her life with, but they didn't. They embraced him because they saw the love and Sumaria was happy with him.

The house hadn't changed a lot from the outside other than it had been painted all white where several years ago, the house had been a dark green. The two large trees in the front yard had grown taller than the house and back when he dated Sumaria, they would spend warm nights sitting under one of the trees talking about the future. Preston felt bad that all the dreams they had didn't pan out the way he'd hoped.

He thought Sumaria would be happy to hear that he was going to stay in Los Angeles and work on being a better man. There was no life for him in Meridian. The jobs paid barely enough for him to afford a roof over his head, even with a roommate. The love of his life deserved a life away from Meridian, something he assumed she found because no one had an inkling of where she lived. Seeing her at the funeral fueled the love he'd never let go of. Sumaria was more beautiful than she had been before and he assumed from the birth of their son, her body was fuller and just as sexy. His desire and deep-seated love her hadn't dwindled one iota. In fact, the moment he saw her, he wanted to lift her into his arms, holding on and never letting go again. That was his purpose for finally coming back to town. He was now the man he wanted to be for her and until she agreed to give him another chance, he was putting his life on hold and now that he had a son, his fate was forever sealed. He was going to fight now just for her love, but for his place in his son's life and as he watched Tara walk back and forth, he was looking at the one person he knew could help him.

Stepping out of the car, he walked across the street hoping that once Tara saw him that she wouldn't turn and walk or run away, perhaps warning Sumaria of his presence if she was here. As he got closer to her, he saw Tara first smile and then she looked at him with a stoic expression that he couldn't read. He approached carefully and hoped she could be an ally, even against her best friend.

"Hi, Tara."

"You shouldn't be here, Prez. I'm serious, you should turn around because Sumaria isn't here and if she was, she wouldn't want to see you. I'm not too keen on seeing you right now myself. What's it been, three years?" she asked him facetiously.

He took her attitude because he deserved it. However, he was trying to make things right.

"I know."

"And you walked away, again, earlier. What is it with you and leaving?"

"Not fair on that one. I tried to talk to her and she didn't want to talk to me. Plus, I needed a moment to take in the fact that I have a son and how that was kept from me."

"Kept from you? Don't just blame her; you didn't come back."

"I didn't know she was pregnant."

"That shouldn't have been the only thing that would have made you come back. Perhaps, that's why she didn't tell you. You hurt her. You really hurt her. She cried for weeks; months and then she had to refocus for Aiden. She was dealing with an ailing father, being pregnant and doing everything on her own. Where were you? Chasing a dollar and a dream."

"I wasn't chasing the dollar, just the dream and I was doing it for her. I tried to reach out for months and she changed her number. I tried to reach her through her parent's number and she changed that number too. She pushed me out of her life completely, but I'm here and I need to see her; I need to talk to her. Where is she, Tara?"

He opened and closed his mouth when one of the guys from the moving company walked up sweating profusely and asked her several questions. The heat of the hot June day had him sweating too, probably for more than just the heat. He was anxious to get to Sumaria.

"She won't see you."

"I'd like to try. Is she still in town? I gave her my number and she hasn't called me."

"She's not going to call."

"Tara, I need to see my son. He doesn't even know me. All I want to do is talk to her. She wouldn't let me explain myself the way I wanted to back then. I don't even know if I could explain it then, but I can now. You know how much I love her and that hasn't changed. Nothing about how I feel about her has changed, unless you want to count seeing her today made me love her even more. I miss her and I need to know if she misses me enough to give me a chance; one small window is all I need," he pleaded.

Preston began to feel hopeful when he watched Tara's shoulders sink in defeat. He was wearing her down."

"She's my best friend. I can't betray that."

He had to come from a different angle.

"Do you have children?" he asked.

When she raised her head and looked him dead in the eyes, he knew he was reaching her. There was no doubt that she was beginning to remember the times she, him and Sumaria would talk about their futures and how they wanted to have kids one day.

"No, but my brother has two kids who I feel like are mine. I'm protective of them and I love them very much."

"Think about this; if you had a child or even your brother's kids and someone kept them from you, how would you feel? If you had a son or daughter of your own, wouldn't you want them to know their father? I don't know that kind of bond between father and child, but you do. You were raised with your parents just as Sumaria was, but not me. I had parents who didn't care about me enough to love me. I never wanted that for any kid of mine and that's something you know. I didn't know about Aiden until yesterday at the cemetery. If I had, yes, I would have come back three years ago and figured out a way to make things work. I wanted it to work out with Sumaria and I still do. Help me. All I'm asking is for a conversation with her. Now, is she still in Meridian? Please," he uttered softly.

"No, she's not here. She left yesterday."

"Where? Where did she go? I'm assuming she left because I showed up."

"Yes, she did. She went home. She lives in Atlanta; we both do. She went back to her life. Like you, she needed to deal with her feelings around you showing back up."

"Atlanta? How long has she been living in Atlanta?"

The night before, he went to the internet and finally looked her up and found an article about her as an up and coming designer in Atlanta who had just won a major contract with a television network. He was angry at himself that over the past two years or so, he had been so busy building his life that he didn't take the time to look her up. It was mainly because he was hurt that she had pushed him away and being all he-man, he figured if she didn't want him, he wouldn't want her, but he did. He fought the urge to look her up.

"She moved after she had Aiden and her father passed away. She took her mother with her and moved when she got a job opportunity."

"Can you help me? I promise you if I talk to her and she tells me that she doesn't want anything to do with me, I will give her that, but I won't walk away from my son. No one can ask me to do that. I would die first. I don't even know him, but I would die or him. He's my son, Tara. Do you know what that means to me? He's my blood. Can you talk to her and see if she'll talk to me?"

Tara was his lifeline. She was his only way to Sumaria. With his own connections, he could probably track her down in Atlanta, but through Tara's support, Sumaria may soften to the idea of talking.

"Three years ago when Sumaria told me she was pregnant, I begged her to tell you. Since that day, I have been begging her to tell you. Every time I look in Aiden's face, I see you and she does too. I've had days of telling her that she's wrong for keeping you from him and not allowing him to know that he has a dad out here who I have no doubt, would love him like crazy. What man couldn't love that adorable little boy. She is my best friend, but I don't agree with how she handled this back then or now. Take out your phone," she said.

Without questioning why, he took his phone out of his pocket.

"Okay," he said.

"I'm going to do something that will probably make her madder at me than she's ever been in her life. The good thing is I'll be here in Meridian for a few more days and she'll have an opportunity to calm down and refocus her anger on you and away from me. Here is her cell number."

Preston typed the number into the phone and felt rejuvenated. He had a new lifeline to his heart.

"I plan to receive and accept every bit of her anger and I'm hoping after that, we can get to a point where we can talk this out. I have to make this work. I need to know if there is any love still left in her heart for me. I came back for her. I never, ever stopped loving her. I thought about her every single day since I've been gone. Every project I've worked on, every dollar I've made, every step in my career I've been able to forge through because of her and my hope that one day, I would be able to earn her love and trust back."

"Prez, her life didn't stop because you were gone. What about what she wants? What about where she is in life?" she asked.

"What are you asking? What are you saying? Is she with someone else?"

His heart hurt with the idea that she could have fallen in love with someone else. In his mind and heart, they were meant for each other and there was no other."

"I'm not going to say anything. You and Sumaria need to talk and you need to get to know your son. Aiden needs his daddy in his life and because I know that you and Sumaria had and probably still could have the perfect love, that's why I'm helping you. I'm still mad at you, but I do understand why you did what you did. I get it because I was there, remember? Yes, she has a life, but at the end of the day, she still loves you and it's up to you to make her believe that she can be in love with you again and that you are in her life to stay; not just because of Aiden, but because, like you just said to me, you came back for her."

"I did and I will. Thank you for this."

Preston turned and started back toward his car.

"Prez," Tara called to him.

He turned back around.

"Aiden and Sumaria are my life and I don't want them hurt. If you're back in our lives and yes, I did say ours, you have to mean it when you say you're back to stay. Is that real? If another opportunity arises, will you leave again? I need to know you're here to and will never walk out on her or them again. Promise me that," she said. "You fight to the death for her. Neither one of you are whole until you're together. Don't tell her I said that."

Preston didn't even hesitate; there was no reason to.

"I'm never, ever leaving again. I can't say that Sumaria will ever love and trust me again, but I plan to make every effort to make up for what I've done; for the time lost. I know that her life wasn't put on hold because I wanted her to wait for me and if all I can get at the end of the day is a relationship with my son, I'll take that. I won't be happy, but I will respect her wishes."

"Do you have plans for the next few days?" she asked.

"Nothing that I can't change, why?"

"Some things are better done in person, don't you think?"

He walked back over to her.

"I do."

"Good."

Preston watched her reach into the bag she had over her shoulder and pull out a post card, handing it to him.

"What's this?"

"Her grand opening coming up in three days, on Saturday. Let me just say that Sumaria has done really well for herself. When she was a few months pregnant with Aiden, she got a job offer to manage the opening of an expansion of an interior design business that was headquartered out of Atlanta. She's taken that, bought out the original owner from life insurance her parents left her and now she's blowing up. You already know she's good with money and her keen eye has helped her build a nice life for herself. I live in Atlanta too and I work in her company. That's where she'll be if you want to talk to her, but don't cause a scene."

"Thanks, Tara. I know you don't have to do this and I appreciate you for giving me a chance to make things right."

"Well, don't thank me yet. If this blows up and doesn't work, it's all your fault. If it works out, name your next child with Sumaria after me."

Preston hugged her tight and knew what his next move would be. Turning and jogging back to his car, he dialed his assistant and the minute she answered, his only instruction was to book him a flight to Atlanta. He was getting his woman back.

6

The best in R&B music played through carefully placed speakers, staff from the hired catering company carried trays of finger foods, wine and champagne and guests were enjoying themselves the way Sumaria had hoped they would. Today was a big day for her and though she'd just gone through a trying time of burying her mother, she had worked hard for this day and wanted everything to be perfect. As she greeted one invited guest after another, she nervously smoothed her hands down her red strapless dress and felt good in her five-inch gold stilettos, matching the colors in the brand for her company, *Sumaiden Designs.*

"You did an amazing job and you look even more beautiful than ever."

She turned around when her attorney and close friend, Hakeem Noland and Tara walked up to her.

"Hakeem, I'm glad you could make it and thank you. You look nice yourself."

"She's beautiful, right?" Tara asked.

"She's gorgeous," Hakeem said and Sumaria blushed at the intense look in his eyes. She would be surprised if it wasn't for the fact that Hakeem had been flirting with her for months and now that her deal was done, she knew what was coming next. He was interested in her and she liked him a lot. He'd asked her out several times and she asked him to give her time to get through all the business and if he still wanted to go out after, she would be open to that. His role in getting her contracts negotiated and signed was done and now they could move from a business relationship to a more personal one. She hadn't dated seriously since moving to Atlanta, but she'd been thinking about it since meeting Hakeem. He was a good guy and his interest in her never wavered.

"I appreciate you both and the turnout is incredible," she proclaimed.

"It's all for you. Where's Aiden? I thought you were thinking of bringing him?" Tara asked.

"I was, but then I knew it would be a long day and he would get cranky. Daytime events are not his deal, especially when that naptime kicks in. He's home with, Maria, the best nanny in the world. I'm just glad both of you are here to hold me up."

"I wouldn't miss your big day as your attorney or as your friend. You've worked hard for this for an entire year and I'm just glad you allowed me to be a part of it."

"I have you to thank for negotiating my contract

and getting me this deal."

When Hakeem leaned closer to her ear, she wasn't sure what he was about to say because suddenly, her eyes were playing tricks on her. She must have been subconsciously thinking about Preston and he was appearing in her every thought and vision because right now, standing near the entrance to the design showroom floor was the man she'd left back in Meridian three days ago. If he's real, what was he doing in Atlanta. He had to be a mirage.

Her assumption went down the drain when he spotted her and started making his way through the throngs of people between the front door and the back of the room where she stood talking to Hakeem after Tara suddenly disappeared. A few people recognized him and stopped his progression with hugs and handshakes, but his eyes never left hers.

She could feel the vein in her neck throbbing as her heart rate sped out of control. Preston was in Atlanta at her grand opening and she had nowhere to run.

"Sumaria?"

She turned to Hakeem when he called her name. Just that fast, she forgot he was standing with her. Her legs felt shaky and her hands felt balmy. Was she sweating? Was she noticeably breathing harder?

"Um, yeah? I'm sorry, what did you say?" she asked, addressing him, but keeping her eyes on Preston who was a few steps away.

"I asked if we could talk privately for a moment,

but you abruptly seem distracted. The look on your face is strange. Are you okay?"

She didn't know what to say. No words could explain the anxiety she was feeling and once Preston walked up to her, she didn't have any time to come up with any.

"Preston? You're here?" she quickly stumbled out. She guessed she found her voice and a few words. When he smiled at her, she knew she should smile back but any expression felt foreign. She felt out of her element with him in her space; in her business; in her town.

"Is that a question or a statement? Yes, I'm here."

She looked between the two men who were looking each other over until both sets of eyes landed on her, undoubted looking for her to do the introductions.

"Oh, um, yeah, Hakeem Noland, this is Preston Washington, an old friend."

There it was. He was an old friend. But was he? It sounded stupid to say it like that and was probably just as bad to their ears. As they shook hands, she took that second to gather herself, finding the entire situation awkward. She was just thinking about what her response would be when Hakeem asked her out and then Preston showed up and any thoughts about Hakeem went out of the window.

"Nice to meet you," they each said.

"Hakeem is my attorney. Um, and my friend. What are you doing here in Atlanta? How did you find out about today?"

Before Preston could answer, she looked beyond him and caught Tara mouthing that she was sorry. She had her answer. She'd deal with Tara later. Turning her attention back to Preston and Hakeem, she inhaled deeply and focused on the issue at hand. She was flanked by two fine men, one who still had her heart and another who would love to have it.

"Preston Washington? Hold up! You're that Preston Washington, the super producer at *Big Fella Records*? I hear you just launched your own label and you already have the new number one recording artist in the country."

"That's me."

Sumaria looked around at all of the people who were now looking their way, surely fans of Preston's and watching Hakeem behave like a crazed fan.

"Sumaria, you didn't tell me you knew Preston, better known as Prez. Wow, this guy has had so many hits over the past year, there is news that he's a sure win for producer of the year at the biggest award show coming up in a few months."

Just as she was about to answer, she closed her mouth and then opened it with shock when Hakeem quickly produced a business card, grinning at Preston with every tooth in his mouth.

"I wasn't expecting him today and it never came up," she said hoping to rejoin the conversation. Watching Hakeem fall all over Preston was taking her back. Yes, Preston was a big star and he was at her event, but he was there for the event.

"Yeah, I thought I would surprise her and come out to support and maybe confer on some set design work for some upcoming videos I'm shooting. I hear she's the go-to person when it comes to taking an idea and making it come to life."

Sumaria was shocked when she saw Hakeem take Preston's hand again and this time, he was vigorously shaking it as if he was trying to shake it off while at the same time, dapping him on the shoulders. What was she witnessing? Hakeem finally stopped when Preston looked at where Hakeem was still holding onto his hand.

"She's definitely the perfect woman for that," Hakeem said. "I was her attorney for the contract that is the cause for today's celebration and our work is done, but I can certainly extend that for any work you'd like to do with her. I would love to talk to you about that and maybe I can be of help on other projects. I'm always looking for an opportunity to pitch what I can do to potential new clients and entertainment law is my specialty. It's why I was assigned to Sumaria at the firm because of the television shows she'll be working with. All of my numbers are on my card. I hope you'll give me a call and since you're in town, maybe we can do lunch and talk business. I would do anything to get you on as a client. Think about it," Hakeem said.

Sumaria wanted Hakeem to stop talking. She knew

the look on Preston's face and knew that he had no plans of giving business to Hakeem and was taking joy in watching him practically foaming at the mouth over his celebrity status. She wanted to die, especially with all of the talking Hakeem was doing, Preston's eyes never left her.

"I'll tell you what, if you give me a moment to chat up Sumaria, I'll find you in the crowd here and we can talk about it. How's that?" Preston asked.

"She's all yours. I'll be close by when you're done. Sumaria, who else are you keeping under your hate on the level of this guy? You've been holding out on a brother," Hakeem exclaimed.

"A few moments?" Preston asked again.

This time, Hakeem leaned over, kissed her on the cheek and walked away after patting Preston on the shoulder.

"You are not going to meet with him and you know it. You shouldn't have given him that kind of hope. What are you doing here?" she asked.

"You left me in Meridian thinking you were going to call me and I see you ran away. What's up with that?" he asked.

"I learned how to run away from the best," she responded shrewdly.

Wishing she hadn't said the words that were floating in her head, she covered her mouth.

"Okay," Preston replied. The confused look on his face told her that he was open to taking her punches like a man.

"I'm sorry. That was uncalled for."

"No worries. I deserved that."

In the next instant, they were joined by two giggling women, both she recognized as cast members of a new reality show coming to Atlanta, one of the three shows where her company was being hired to design the sets.

"Prez, can we get your autograph?" one of them said.

"Can I get your phone number?" the other asked and they collectively giggled again.

"I can definitely get you the autograph, but not the phone number," he said taking the paper one of them held and signed his name to the back of it.

"Can we get a picture?"

"Give me a few minutes, and I promise I'll take a picture with you. I'll even repost it on my IG account for the envy of your friends. Promise you'll give me a minute," he said.

"We promise," they said together and then happily walked away, more like hopped away.

"That's going to keep happening unless you have a place we can talk privately."

Sumaria turned and walked with Preston close behind her. Without talking, she entered through several doors and a doorway until they reached her lavish office in the back of the building.

"Wow! This is nice. Where did you find this gold

and glass desk?"

Instead of answering, she closed the door behind them and lowered the blinds that would generally give her staff an eye view of activity in her office. The large, open floor plan of the office space was her idea because she wanted them to operate as a team with a family feeling. For now, she needed privacy though no one was in the open office area. They were all out front celebrating.

"Why are you here, Preston?"

"Okay, so no chitchat. I got you. Can I sit down?" he asked.

She pointed to her red leather sofa and when he sat, she walked around to the front of her desk and leaned back on it, bracing her hands on the edge. She was so nervous that she needed something steady to grip and hold on to.

"I wasn't expecting to see you," she said.

"I got that from the look on your face when you saw me. You should have expected that I would show up one day. I found out I have a son. Did you think that would be it and that I would go back to my life? Really? You know me better than that."

"I thought I knew you, but I didn't, did I?"

"You're equating how you feel about what I did to keeping me away from my son? If no one else knows me, you do and you know that you should have done everything to tell me about him. I never would have been out of my son's life all this time. Were you that pissed at me that you would do that out of spite?"

"I didn't do anything out of spite. I let you live your life. I let you chase your riches because that's what you chose."

Were they really arguing? This was her chance to really let him have it, but her desire for him was greater than her anger at his appearance in her life again.

"No, I chose going after the man I needed to be for you, but mostly, for me. I was half a man back then. Yes, things would have been different if I had known you were pregnant."

"So, you would have come back if you knew I was pregnant, but not just for me?"

When Preston stood and walked toward her, she held her ground even though her body screamed for him the same way her mind doing in her head, blinding her of how tough she was trying to be.

"Baby, I am back for you."

"No, you're here for Aiden."

"No, I found out about Aiden and yes, I want to see my son, but my return was for you. I came for you and whether you believe that or not is up to you."

Sumaria huffed in annoyance. Why couldn't he just stay away and let her live her life with memories without having the real him in front of her and having old feelings resurfacing against her deep-seated desire to not want him. Still, she held firm.

"I don't believe you."

"Listen, I didn't come here to argue and if you want

to bash me again and again because I left you, then go ahead and do that. I can't force you to understand that doing what I did was because I loved you. I know I didn't do it the right way, but I can't go back and change that, just as you can't go back and tell me about my son. I also don't want to keep you from your event and all of your guests who are probably wondering where you are. I came because I want to see Aiden and I want to talk more with you."

"Talk to me about what? You said you want to see Aiden. You sure you don't want me to take some paternity test or something?"

Preston laughed and she was now embarrassed. She knew she sounded childish the minute the words came out.

"Don't even try that."

"Stop laughing at me," she mumbled.

"I'm not laughing at you. I'm laughing at the notion of me asking you to take a paternity test. Don't do that. I know you better than that. Number one, you would never say he's mine if he wasn't and number two, he looks just like me. His parentage is undeniable."

"Okay, so you want to see Aiden; fine. We can set something up for you to see him. Anything else?" she asked, trying to be hard while already knowing she was failing miserably because her body was on fire. She'd never seen him look so good and smell so good and walk and behave with so much confidence. It was sexy and she was turned on like never before. Damn, him, she thought.

Preston was moving; slow, but he was moving and he was coming straight for her. His eyes; those eyes did things to her and her body remembered him. She wanted to rub her legs together to ease the strain between them, having him close to her. He came so close that his minty, heated breath brushed across her nose. If he came a little further, she was imagining a kiss; the kiss that she'd spent many days and nights dreaming about, fantasizing about having again and now with him appearing more mature and damn near erotic the way he was looking at her, she was close to giving him anything he wanted; and she meant anything.

Damn him for knowing how good he was at reminding he how good they were together.

She didn't move when he placed his hands over hers where she held onto the edge of her desk, still leaning against it and when she thought he was really going to kiss her and she would have seconds to either move out of reach or give into her own desire to be kissed by him, he went beyond her lips and went straight for her ear.

"I know you're mad at me and you have every right to be, but damn if you are not the sexiest woman to ever walk the earth. I still love and want you with a passion that no one else other than you could ever make me feel. Be careful when you ask me if I want anything else because I'm not sure if the response I will give would be a respectable one, at least not in this setting. If there is ever anything else I can do for you, all you have to do is ask. Since you did ask, however, I will settle for this."

The kiss came out of nowhere, but the way her body melted under the caress of his lips, it was very much wanted and needed. Her head was spinning as he deepened the kiss and they moaned into each other's mouths. The minute her lips parted a little, he encouraged them open even more and the way his tongue searched out hers, she thought that her mind and body would explode where she sat. She was already close and they were doing was kissing.

Her head was screaming for more, remembering the out-of-this world sex that would often precede and follow a kiss this heated. Just as she was ready to beg for more while her mind wondered how fast she could get undressed and tame the ache between her legs, the kiss ended abruptly. She wanted to scream at him to not pull away, but to continue to kiss her senseless. She looked at him puzzled and then she heard it.

Someone had joined them and cleared their throat. She snapped her head around and her eyes landed on Hakeem who stood with his mouth gaping open at the sight before him. When Preston leaned away from her and wiped her lipstick from his lips, she stood up straight and smoothed her dressed down as her body attempted unsuccessfully to calm.

"Uh, sorry for interrupting, but your name is being called. Everyone's looking for you to give a speech, welcoming your guests. Should I tell them you'll need a moment?" Hakeem asked. There was no doubt he was trying to figure out what he'd just walked in on.

When he looked from her to Preston and then back to her, she didn't know what to say and knew that for a moment, she'd lost her head and the last thing she wanted to do was hurt Hakeem. She didn't know how to explain what he'd just seen.

"How..how long were you standing there?" she asked, moving away from her desk toward where he stood at the door.

"Long enough to know that you're going to need new lipstick since what you had on your lips is now on his. I'll let Tara know you're on your way, should I say in a few seconds, minutes, perhaps an hour if you need more time?"

She could tell from his tone that the sight of Preston making love to her mouth was unsettling. She wouldn't dare apologize because being sorry was far from what she was feeling. Damn Preston for reminding her of his hold over her.

"No, no, I'm coming now," she uttered hurriedly.

Shoot she thought. She hated when a double-entrende entered her conversation. "I mean, I'm on my way right now," she said, cleaning up her words along with her thoughts. Behind her, she heard Preston chortle and turned, practically growling at him for making light of what just happened regarding her embarrassment over being caught.

"Sorry," Preston said and then she caught him laughing again. He wasn't doing it openly, but she saw it in his eyes. She then turned to Hakeem to finally apologize, but before she could, he had disappeared and her office door closed.

"Why did you do that?" she blasted out loud in anger, more at herself than at Preston. She didn't have to let him kiss her.

"Do what? Chuckle or kiss you?"

"Preston, you cannot just waltz in here and kiss me like that. You said you wanted to talk. You said nothing about kissing."

"Okay, I'm sorry. You're so fine, I couldn't resist. I have dreamed about kissing you like that again. I'm sorry if kissing me is such a horrible act. I promise to not do it again unless you ask me to and I hope you will."

That voice; that tone. Her body sizzled. She was in trouble.

"I didn't say that."

"Okay, can I kiss you again now?"

She was confused and the smug look on Preston's face told her he knew what he was doing.

"Stop it! I have to go out there," she said and turned to the door.

"Don't forget your lipstick is smudged."

"Ugh, I forgot about it that quick. Tara has my bag. Are you coming?" she asked and then she heard it again and stopped him when she saw that sly-like, yet sexy look on his face just as he was about to comment. "Don't you dare," she warned.

He held up his hands in surrender and she huffed in irritation at him.

"Okay, I was thinking it, but I won't say it and no, I'm not going back out. I'm going to sit right here until you're done and I'd like to go with you so that I can see my son. I can't chance you running out on me again."

"I'm going to kill Tara. She told you right? Your being here isn't a coincidence and you didn't suddenly decide to look me up and show up here out of the blue?"

"Don't be mad at her. I pulled on her heartstrings pretty hard."

"What, you're just going to sit here and wait? I don't know how long I'll be and Aiden may be asleep by the time I get home. Perhaps another day would be better."

She saw his face and her first thought was, wrong answer, and she knew it.

"Sumaria, you're not doing this to me. I need to see my son and if he's asleep, that's fine. I can stand and watch him sleep, but I want to see him. Don't take that from me. I promise not to press anything else, but please let me see him tonight."

Gone was the smirk that had been on his face when they were caught by Hakeem. Replacing it was the look of a man who was begging and pleading and even with her anger over what happened in the past, now that he was here, she would never keep Aiden from him again.

"Since you're going to wait, are you hungry? I can have someone bring you something to eat or if you want, you can come out to the event. I know you only came because you wanted to see Aiden. Still, it's a party."

"I came for you."

He kept saying that and each time, she wondered how true he was being. Perhaps he had known about Aiden before seeing her at the cemetery.

"I know, you keep saying that."

"I'm going to keep saying it until you hear me and not question my motive."

This time, she let it go. There was no need to belabor where they differed on his purpose. After that kiss, she didn't know why she was questioning anything.

"Okay. Food?" she asked again.

"No, I'm good. I'm going to make a few calls and check some emails."

She turned toward the door and then turned back.

"How long will you be in Atlanta? I know you have work to get back to," she asked.

"As long as it takes."

"For what?"

"Are you and Hakeem an item?"

Surprise, she thought. Where had that come from? What did he pick up on? She was hesitant to talk about Aiden or about their past, but the idea of discussing Hakeem came from left field. Here was another topic that she hoped would fade away. The look on Hakeem's face wasn't only obvious to her, it was to Preston too. What could she possibly say in the few seconds she had before she needed to get back out to her party?

"What?"

"You heard me. Are you seeing Hakeem? Has he been a figure in my son's life in my absence? I want to know what I'm dealing with."

"What difference does that make?" she questioned and then knew it was only because she felt defeated, like he had the upper hand and she wanted to win and maybe get more time to think about everything if he was left wondering and decided to get up and leave out of anger or perhaps jealousy. No, she wouldn't do that to him. She was still harboring old hurt, but he didn't deserve having her play with his feelings.

"No, I'm not seeing him and he's not a figure in Aiden's life. He's a friend."

"Who's in love with you."

"I wouldn't say that."

"Did you not see the look on his face? Oh, he's definitely in love with you and I can't blame him. What I want to know is what does he mean to you?"

"He's my attorney and my friend; that's it."

"Okay, ask me your question again?"

"What question?"

"The last one you asked."

Sumaria thought back and then remembered. She wasn't sure she wanted the answer.

"How long will you be in Atlanta?"

When Preston looked up from his phone where he had been pecking away even while questioning her about Hakeem, he didn't raise his head fully, but his eyes zeroed in on hers and she feared looking away. She needed the way he looked at her. She wanted the way he looked at her. She'd been waiting a long time to have him look at her and now that she had it, the intensity was unsettling while also deeply satisfying.

"Until I have my woman back."

She opened her mouth to counter and didn't. She walked out of her office and left him sitting there. How could she respond when she wanted him so bad that if he asked her to slip out of the party and join him back at his hotel, she would already be leaving with him. She needed a clearer mind. Could she believe that he came back for her?

Rushing to get back to her guests, she was greeted at the door just before entering the main showroom. She didn't have to say anything in response to what she saw; Tara with a wide grin on her face and a tube of her favorite *Fenty* lipstick in her hand.

"Need this?"

Sumaria looked around for Hakeem and saw him near the front door talking to a group of guests.

"Hakeem told you?"

"You bet your sweet *ass* he did. He told me that if he hadn't interrupted, Preston would have taken you right there on the desk. That hot, huh? Y'all still have that spark, that fire? You are a dirty, dirty girl and I love it! I have a condom if you need it," Tara said and doubled over in laughter.

"You're a sad person making fun of your best friend like this. Give me the lip stick."

"Absolutely. You back there in your office making hot girl moves and lost your lip stick. Still have your panties on?" Tara joked.

Sumaria gritted her teeth, not in anger, but in embarrassment. Over the years, when Preston's name would come up in their conversations, she would be cold and unwavering in her distaste for any thought or words about him. Even then, Tara knew she was lying, but like a best friend would do, she played off as if she didn't. She needed that Tara right now.

"Stop it. He caught me off-guard. I didn't know he was going to kiss me or kiss me like that. It was incredible and rather intoxicating. He feasted on me like I was a Thanksgiving meal."

"Did you stop him or did you show him you could still give as good as you got?"

"Not now, Tara. I need to refocus and get my body in check," she admitted.

"Damn, that good? All he did was kiss you?"

"Tara!"

"Okay, okay, I'll stop for now."

"Cover for me for a second so I can put on my lip stick. How hurt was Hakeem?" she asked.

"Crushed. He asked me about you and Prez, but I

didn't tell him. You're going to have to tell him yourself after you figure out which guy you want. Imagine that. A few days ago, you had no man and today, you have two lusting after you. If I didn't have a man, I would love to be in your position right now. Who will the lucky guy be? If you ask my opinion..."

"I'm not asking your opinion and there is no choice to make."

"But, if you were to ask me, I'm team Prez, just so you know. That man has always loved you and I know he left you, but you have to understand why; you have to. Think about that, think about Aiden and then think about how you're still in love with him. Be that happy. I'll stall everyone while you go fix yourself up. You're flushed. Still thinking about that kiss and a little bit more, perhaps?"

She would have responded, but Tara walked away, leaving her to ponder what she was really feeling. She looked in Hakeem's direction and when he gave her a smile and a slight wave, she knew she needed to address the elephant in the room between them. That would come later. She needed to get back to her celebration and then deal with Preston.

7

He has a son. He has a whole son! His son. He had a little him in the world. Over and over again in his head, Preston said that to himself. As he looked down into Aiden's crib as he slept, he was overwhelmed with an abundance of love and protection. In fact, before he could realize what was happening to him, his heart exploded with more love than he ever thought he could find within himself. This was it; this was love. For the past few days, he tried to process it all. Since the moment he saw Aiden and Sumaria admitted he was his father, nothing else in his life mattered other than loving Sumaria and having his son in his arms; being a part of his life.

Aiden was asleep on his stomach with his legs hunched up under him in a white one-piece pajama set with zoo animals all over it. Reaching down, he lightly ran his hands over Aiden's full head of dark brown curly hair.

"He's perfect," he whispered.

Looking around the room, Aiden's bedroom was the perfect child's room with its dark brown crib, dresser and rocking chair. There was a three-shelf bookcase filled with books, two large plastic brown storage boxes, no doubt filled with toys and in big dark brown wood lettering in the center of the wall above the crib was Aiden's name spelled out against the wall painted in mint green. Next to a window, he saw a closet and was sure it was filled with clothes. The room was a clear reflection of Sumaria and Aiden and nothing of him. The reality of missing years with was a punch to his gut. When his eyes landed on Sumaria standing at the bedroom door, still in her red party dress, but now in her bare feet, he wanted to be angry for the time he missed, but he couldn't. He still loved her so much and there was no way to change the past. Dwelling on it had no purpose.

"He really is perfect," she replied. "He's a happy little boy who loves toy trucks, plastic zoo animals and running. He went straight from crawling to running with no in-between."

He heard her humor and was glad it replaced her anger from earlier in the day. He turned back to Aiden and just watched him. So many feelings ran through him and the days of his own youth stood out.

There was no love in his life from his mother or father. His father was in an out of his life as a little boy and then as he grew, he found his father slipping into the small apartment late at night where he lived with his mother but by morning, he would be gone. That was a pattern for the man he longed to have a relationship with. He would draw him pictures and bring home projects from school he made so that he could show him and hopefully get some kind words or any recognition, but he never did. His mother showed little concern and often told him that he was a mistake but at least she was paid by the state to keep him around. That was the story of his life. As he became a man and fell in love with Sumaria, he knew they would get married and have their own kids one day and he vowed that he would shower his kids with so much love that they would get tired of hearing it and feeling it and would know that he would always be there for him.

"A little track star he is, huh?" he joked.

"He's a good, feisty little guy."

"You've done good. You didn't have to do this without me. I wish you have given me the chance to know him from birth. Us being together or not shouldn't have been a factor. My son," he said again, not talking to Sumaria but communicating that to Aiden even in his sleep.

"Prez, I'm sorry. I know I was wrong and I don't know what to do or say that could take away the hurt of the time you missed with him."

"You called me Prez just now. I guess that a step up from you calling me Preston. You used to do that when you were angry with me. Did you not tell me about him because you were angry at me for not coming back? Were you really going to raise my son and never tell me about him? What if I hadn't gone to Meridian for your mother's funeral? We have a lot to talk about and I'm hoping it's not getting too late that you're not up to talking tonight. I have a lot of questions, but right now, I just want to stand here and look at my son while he sleeps. Is that okay with you? I won't wake him."

Alone time. That's all he wanted. That's all he needed at this moment. So much of his life had no purpose until it did and right now, nothing else seemed to matter other than living in the moment with his eyes on his son.

"I didn't keep Aiden from you out of spite or anger. Yes, I was hurt that you didn't come back, but I didn't try to subconsciously hurt you by keeping Aiden a secret. It's hard to explain that when I first found out I was pregnant, I didn't know what to do and yes, I was still hurt, barely sleeping, no appetite and you were doing what you said you needed to do and I decided to let you. I was planning on telling you before I had Aiden, but with my dad getting worse, that became the focus and then I went into labor. I was going to call you and every time I tried, I couldn't complete the call. My focus then became taking care of Aiden while working and looking after my father. It was a lot and I didn't process it well. It's not an excuse, it's just how it was. I'm really sorry. I swear I am."

"Don't keep my son from me anymore. We need to

figure this out. I love you and I forgive you because I see my son and I know the strain the stress between two parents can have on a child. I don't want that for him. In all of this, I love you and there's a lot we need to talk about. Any idea you have of keeping him from me is done. I'm here and I'm not going anywhere. If you don't want me, no longer love me or want to have nothing to do with me and I can't change your mind, you have every right to have your life, but this is my son and he doesn't know me. Do you know what that feels like? You can't know. You didn't have my life. Just don't keep my son from me. You know I don't have any family; I never really had any, but him? He's mine."

Preston could hear his own voice breaking as he spoke. There was so much emotion floating through him and he was struggling to take it all in. He didn't know what her true motive was and he wasn't about to dissect it as if the missing time would come back and he could relive the moment of seeing Aiden being born.

When Aiden shifted, grunted and moaned in his sleep as if he couldn't find a comfortable position, on instinct, Preston rubbed his back softly and watched him calm.

"Let's talk when you're ready. Spend some time here with Aiden and I'll be downstairs in the family room. I'm going to make me some hot chocolate. Would you like some?"

"Sure. I'll be down in a bit."

He heard Sumaria's feet padding away on the wood

floor and he exhaled. He didn't know what was going to happen next, but if begging and pleading would work, he'd try that. Sumaria and Aiden were his family and he needed his family in his life.

Moving the rocking chair so that he could sit and still be close to Aiden, he sat down and slipped his fingers through the slats of the crib. Something about touching his son's skin made him feel even more connected. The moment was serene and it was this moment when he knew, no matter what Sumaria would decide when it came to them, getting on that plane to Meridian was the best decision he'd ever made; it was the right time.

He had struggled with what to do knowing that since the moment he left Meridian and caused the end of his relationship with Sumaria, he knew he would one day go back to try and make things right with her. He knew he ran the risk of her being involved with someone or even married, but he was willing to risk that because he had to know. She was his world, then and still now. Together with Aiden, they were all the family he had. He had friends and even those who treated him like family, but in his heart, he had no one, but his heart still held her.

Closing his eyes, he dropped his head and took in the weight of the moment and then he felt movement from Aiden and he looked back up where their eyes locked. Neither of them moved, but Aiden reached for his hand and grabbed his thumb and held on. He didn't know what to do, but if Aiden held his finger like this until the end of time, he wouldn't move a muscle.

"Hey little man. You're supposed to be sleep."

Preston was startled when he saw Aiden's lips quiver as if he was about to cry.

"No, no, no. Your mommy is going to go ballistic if she thinks I woke you up. I know you don't know me, but please don't cry. I'm new at this."

From the look on Aiden's face, he was unaware of how they were connected and though he didn't know him, his son still held tight to his thumb.

Preston stood up and Aiden began to whimper. He started to call for Sumaria, but he didn't. Instead, he leaned over, taking his hand out of Aiden's grip and tried to rub his back to get him back to sleep. Aiden's eyes were focused on his every move and he wondered if he was processing who the stranger was who was comforting him and if in the next second, he would belt out a cry in terror over not seeing Sumaria.

None of that happened. Instead, he watched Aiden move around until he was sitting up and then it happened. Aiden's arms reached out and without hesitation, he picked him up into his arms.

"Hey, hey. You're okay. You may not know it, but you're okay."

When Aiden rested his head on his chest, Preston sat down in the rocking chair and lifted him up on his shoulders. He'd never held a child this small before, but on instinct, he rested Aiden's head in the crook of his neck, rubbed his back and without singing the words, he hummed the song of one of his artists whose words he would not say out loud. The humming somehow soothed Aiden and so together, they sat, father and son, bonding. Aiden wasn't afraid of him. And just like that, he was back to sleep. He started to put him back in his crib, but waited. This moment was as perfect as they came and he wouldn't give it up for anything – even Sumaria's wrath if she walked in and found him holding him. Before the end of the night, they would need to figure out how to deal with the role he plans to play in his son's life and hopefully in her life too.

~~

Hakeem sat outside of Sumaria's house and waited. How long he'd wait, he wasn't sure, but inside was the woman he was hoping to get to know on a more personal level, but today, there was a shift in the air between them and it happened with the arrival of Preston "Prez" Washington, the music industry's golden super producer.

He was still trying to wrap his head around where had he come from. One minute, he was sharing small moments of flirting with Sumaria and the next, he found her practically on the verge of being naked and getting busy in her office with the man and that came out of nowhere. How did she know Prez? How long have they been that close? The way they were kissing, they were familiar with each other and like some voyeur, he'd stood watching as if he was viewing a scene in a movie. The kiss was hot and amorous, something even he could see. It was the kind of kiss he was planning on sharing with her now that he was no longer working on her case. Instead, he found himself in stalker mode at nine in the evening.

When he left the daytime celebration of Sumaria's business expansion, he headed for home; alone. His day had started out well. He had stopped by his office early enough to catch another lawyer at the firm so that he could turn over all of Sumaria's files to her. He'd made it known that he had more than a professional interest in the beauty back when her case was first given to him after her previous lawyer quit the firm and took a job someplace else. His first meeting with Sumaria was something out of a romance movie. He sat waiting for her in the firm's conference room and when the door opened and his assistant escorted her in, his mouth dropped, the temperature in the room rose by a thousand degrees and he couldn't take his eyes off of how stunning she was.

She had been impeccably dressed in a dark green pants suit that hugged her body in all the right places. Her long hair was down flowing around her shoulders with the addition of her gold and green jewelry and nails designed to match, she was walking perfection. He remembered feeling stupid when she introduced herself, held her hand out for him to shake and he didn't move; not to shake her hand, not to say a word or to pull out her chair. He stood like a panting dog ogling everything about her. His assistant had to break the trance by speaking and telling Sumaria who he was. He was embarrassed, but Sumaria let him off the hook graciously. He tried to keep things professional over the months of them working together until he couldn't hold back his interest in her any longer. She made it clear to him that she couldn't cross that line with him as long as he was her attorney. One day, he asked if he could take her out on a real date after he completed the negotiation of her contracts and then turned her over to another lawyer at the firm. He explained his rationale that over the months of them working closely together, his attraction to her steadily grew. He wanted to know if they could be something more. He wouldn't hand her over to just any lawyer at the firm, but to someone he trusted to do as good a job and look out for her interest in the same way that he would. He even brought the subject up to those he answered to at the firm and everyone pretty much gave him the same response; they already knew he had feelings for her and keeping her business at the firm was the priority. Whatever direction Sumaria wanted to go in, they would support it. The idea was to keep the client happy.

Two weeks ago, when his work was done, they spoke about going out on an official date sometime after her event. She wanted to get through that and he knew how stressful pulling that off was, so he stood back and gave her the space she needed.

All bets were off when he watched her enter the

showroom event earlier in the day. He could hear his own heart beating in his chest. He couldn't wait for the day when she would be on his arm as his woman. Since the event only served hors d'oeuvres, he decided to make dinner reservations for them at one of the best restaurants in Atlanta just in case she agreed to go out with him that night. That's how anxious he was to move to the next level with her. Then, everything changed when he walked back to her office where he assumed, she would be alone, but that wasn't the case.

The world tilted when he watched her enjoying her lip-lock with Preston. At first, he was intrigued and then furious. He had been lost in the moment of how intimate their kiss was. It wasn't their first time and she was more than enjoying it. He watched her and, in her actions, not words, she was begging for more. He could see it.

He was in love with Sumaria and he admired how Prez had come from nothing to be the most sought-after music producer in the industry. Still, the man was kissing the woman he wanted to have in his arms. For the rest of the night, he watched Sumaria and though Preston didn't show back up at the event, he knew she was thinking about him. Several times, he caught her looking toward the hallway to her office where he assumed Preston stayed. At the end of the evening when most guests had left and only the crew who were cleaning up were there along with Tara who was giving instructions, he walked over to finally get a word with

Sumaria and that's when he noticed the final shift in their relationship or the lack of one now or in the future.

His first question was to ask her about her relationship with Preston and her only response was that it was complicated. He hated when people said that and thought it was an answer to a direct question that should have an easy answer. When he asked her what her complicated connection to Preston meant for the two of them, she again uttered that it was all complicated. Before he could press her any further, Preston walked up with a cocky look on his face and all conversation stopped. Sumaria looked like she was about to say something, but seeing the way she was looking at Preston and the way he was nearly undressing her with just a look her way, he didn't give her the chance. He turned and walked away to chat briefly with Tara and out of the corner of his eye, he watched Sumaria disappear toward the back with Preston again. She gave one last expressionless look his way and then walked off. This time, he wouldn't set himself up to get an eyeful. He said goodbye to Tara and he left.

Here he now was, after driving around without thinking where he was going, he ended up parked on her street, one house down from hers. When he first pulled up, he had planned to ring the bell to try and talk to her to find out where he stood with her and then he saw an unfamiliar car on the side of her house in front of the garage doors and knew that it could only be Preston.

How could he not know that she was seeing someone and that someone was one of the most recognizable faces on the planet? When had they started seeing each other and why wouldn't she tell him when he expressed his own interest in her? He jumped through a lot of hoops to finally be able to be in a relationship with her, something he thought they were on the same page with, but clearly, he had been the one in the dark.

When he should have driven away, he didn't. He sat like some lost puppy wondering what was going on inside of the house. Was her son there? Had Preston been to her house before? Were there more kisses? Touching? Making out? Were they having sex? The idea of another man touching her before he got his chance fueled his anger at her and Preston. How could he allow himself to be played like this? He had a lot of questions, but he wouldn't get the answers he sought on this night. His rage began to boil over. The last woman he tried to be involved with had played him like this, but that time, it had been with one of his closest friends. What he had walked in on with them was much more than just kissing like he'd seen with Sumaria and Preston. That moment haunted him and now, another woman was choosing another man over him.

Letting his fury loose, he pounded his fists as hard as he could on the dashboard of his car. Again and again he pulverized the hard leather until his fists hurt and a man walking a dog along the sidewalk looked his way. He quickly calmed, gave the man a polite wave and when he continued on with his dog, he put his car back in drive and slowly drove past her house.

Tomorrow was another day and like his original plan for tonight, he was going to show up again. This time, he would talk to her and remind her that she promised him dinner and he was going to hold her to it whether she wanted to or not. He was no match for who Preston was but he cared about her and he wanted her to be his; Preston or not.

8

Sumaria was sipping her hot chocolate when Preston finally came down the stairs from Aiden's room. She thought about going up to check on him because he'd been gone for so long, almost an hour since she'd come downstairs, leaving them alone. He looked so sad, yet happy and she wanted to continue to apologize again and again for not telling him he was a father, but there was no use. If she thought she was going to be able to buy more time like she did when she high-tailed it out of Meridian, that was far from the case. Preston was now in her house and she knew the day of reckoning was upon her.

"I thought maybe you'd fallen asleep up there. Is he still asleep?" she asked when he came into the room and sat down. She curled her legs under her to hide her edginess. They were alone now; what would she say?

She held back any more words when he leaned his head all the way back on the top of the sofa and closed his eyes. The silence was deafening not knowing what was going through his head. She was ashamed and kicked herself for the time Aiden lost with him because of her selfishness. What could she say that would make up for what she did? Her eyes locked on the way he sat, with his legs open and planted solidly on the floor. He shirt was unbuttoned by an extra button and she admired the platinum bracelet on his wrist. In this moment, she could really get a good look at him and how he'd changed in a few short years.

Besides new muscles that were everywhere and noticeable with his short-sleeved shirt, he had let his hair grow out on top where the same curls that Aiden had were also on his head. The sides were trimmed short and he was growing a beard which added to his debonair looks.

Preston had always been handsome and still just as sexy and desirable as he ever was. How could she have denied herself of possibly being with him for so long?

That was her thinking when he leaned up and looked over at her. She prepared herself for his rage.

"He's sleeping, but he did wake up briefly. I thought he was going to scream to the heavens when he saw me, a complete stranger standing over him. I had my hand on the bed right next to him and he reached for my thumb and held it tight. His face got this look that I thought was telling me to get out of his face, but instead, he reached his arms out to me and I picked him up in my arms. He stared in my face as if he was trying to figure out who I was. I was afraid to even breathe because I didn't know what was next. If he started bawling, I was going to scream for you. I didn't want him terrorized. Slowly, he lowered his head to my chest and squirmed around like he was trying to get comfortable; he even whimpered a bit. I let him move however he wanted and then I sat down. When I did that, I lifted him further and he laid his head on my shoulder, patted my face and held on to it. I started humming a song lightly, hoping that would settle him back down. After a few minutes when his hand dropped, I knew he'd fallen back asleep. I took so long because I sat there holding him. I didn't want to put him down. It took everything in me to not sit there like that all night long. He needs his sleep so I put him back down. The best moment of my life! Holding my son! You can't know how I feel right now; you can't know."

She couldn't and she wouldn't try. That was his time with Aiden and she could look at him and know that it's not only what he needed or even what Aiden needed, but now she knew, this is what she needed. She needed him to meet his son. Before today, it had been a dream. The reality was much, much better.

"What do you want me to say?" she asked.

"At this point, I don't even know. I want to be angry, but I can't be because you are so damn beautiful and sexy and I still love you so much even after this. I can't be mad at you though I want to be. I want to say that I didn't deserve being kept in the dark. Yes, I didn't come back for you three years ago, but he's my son, Sumaria; he's my son and I should have known. Were you really going to let my son walk through life and never know that I was out here? I don't understand how you couldn't think about that or think about what his life would be like without his father. Do you not remember what I went through? Remember how I wanted nothing more than for my father to say he loved me, wanted me, hell, even cared that I existed?"

She wanted to reach for Preston's hand to soothe his hurt, but what she wouldn't be able to stand would be his rejection at this moment. When she started to reach for him, she grasped her cup tighter.

"I didn't know how you would feel if I called and said, oh yeah, even though you didn't choose me, I'm pregnant with your child so you have to come back now. I didn't get pregnant on purpose. You know we used protection all the time; well, most of the time. He wasn't planned, but I didn't want my pregnancy to be the reason you came back for me. I didn't then and I don't want that now. Think of how different your life would have turned out if you had come back to Meridian. I hear your worth is around forty million dollars right now. You and Anthony have made it and I'm happy it all worked out for you. This is what you wanted. You wanted to be a celebrity. You wanted stardom. You wanted the mogul status. You wanted to be rich."

"Really, Sumaria? That's what you think was or is

important to me? Yes, I went in search of my dreams, but I always thought my steps would include you. Never did I think we would end over me going after my dreams. You left Meridian to go to college in Florida and I celebrated you. I felt alone when you left and I visited you when I could come up with enough money to take the trip. I would be sitting on your front steps when I knew your father had driven to Florida to pick you up from school. I didn't have much, but I had you and you had me. You gave up on us, on me when I needed your support. You wouldn't hear me back then, but I had to do it, baby; I had to."

"I hear you now. I'm sorry I wasn't understanding and supportive. I played a game with what we were and I lost. I lost you; I lost us and I've lived with the regret of that since then. Then I had Aiden – a piece of you and I loved him. Every time he looked at me and smiled or even laughed, he was all you and I had that piece of you that I needed in order to get through another day after you left. It was hard and I was selfish for making you have to choose. I wanted you to choose me and you didn't and that was crushing."

She was on the brink of crying for all the times she cried and didn't have him with her. Like a wish from a dream, he was here now and how was she going to go back to him not being hers? She held back her tears when he slid closer, took her cup from her hands and placed it on the table before taking both of her hands in to his.

"We can't go back and we can't live in that time. Those were the best times of my life and then they weren't. I have made major achievements in my life and it's all material and superficial. I have it and I don't splurge. There were too many years in the past where if it weren't for you and your family, I wouldn't have had decent meals; ever. I have a car, a condo and some nice pieces of jewelry and clothes. You know I had to have clothes after I spent years admiring others from a distance when they got the latest sneakers or other clothes and shoes and I couldn't. I invest well, but close to me was always the desire and love for you. I never let go of that and it took me a long time to get up the nerve to come in search of you to see if there was any chance that we could try again. The last thing on my mind are all those things I just mentioned that are material and replaceable. What's not replaceable is you and now Aiden. Those things are nice and my worth financially isn't worth having if I'm enjoying it without you and him. It's not about that and what you heard about my worth is quite a bit more than that. Stop reading social media."

"I didn't mean to make you think I was saying you are only about the material. I know it was what you were working hard to get. That's all I'm saying. You reached that. You're successful, so moving to L.A. when you did was worth it."

How could she really explain how proud of him she was without insulting him with thoughts that he didn't care about her in all of that.

"None of it is worth anything. I didn't know what to do after so much time had passed. When Anthony told me he heard about your mother's funeral being in town, something told me that was my chance. I had come back once before about a year before that and someone was renting your parents' house and he didn't have any information on you. I probably could have found you if I wanted to, but when I started to think through locating you, I didn't want to invade your privacy and the space you wanted from me. I never changed my number, though you changed yours. I wanted you to be able to reach me if you wanted to. I figured you didn't want to be a part of my life and had moved on. I took a chance anyway because as much as I tried to move on, I couldn't. To now know that I have a son, I know I was meant to go back to Meridian when I did. Are you at least a little happy to see me? A smidgen? Remember your mother used to say that word all the time? It took me a while to understand what that word meant."

Preston was smiling. That was a good sign. Their conversation didn't have to be heavy and they could get through it without anybody being left hurt. He said he had come back for her and she needed to stop doubting that truth. She had her own truth.

"I missed you something terrible. Many, many nights I lay alone and wondered what you were doing, who you were with, if you even cared about me anymore. I can't help but think about you every day because I have Aiden."

"But you were ready to let him live a life without knowing about me? I don't understand that."

She could rationalize it either, but she knew pictures could tell a thousand stories that she couldn't tell.

"Give me a minute," she said, jumping up and running back up to Aiden's room. When she got there, she checked to be sure he was still sleeping soundly and went to the top shelf of his closet and took down the large photo album she'd started putting together when Aiden was first born. Taking it, she rushed back down the stairs holding it tight in her arms as if it was gold. To her, it was one of the most precious items in her house. She sat back down and faced him.

"What's that?" he asked her.

She was so excited, her thoughts were all over the place. She calmed to explain.

"Prez, I never had any intention of keeping Aiden in the dark when it came to who you are. You said he woke up and saw you and didn't scream like he was looking at Freddy Krueger because trust me, he's not very fond of strangers at all, especially if he doesn't see me. He wasn't afraid because he recognized you. He knows your face."

When Preston's eyes widened and then turned questionable, she knew he didn't understand.

"What? How?" he asked.

"This."

Handing over the photo album she waited for his initial reaction, especially when he read the words on the outside.

"Aiden Preston Washington," he said out loud.

He looked up at her and then back down at the album and then back up at he again.

"Yes. He has your name."

"You gave him my name?"

"I did because you're his father. The picture on the cover was taken a few minutes after he was born. I know people don't really keep photo albums anymore, but I wanted him to know about his life before a time when he would remember it and I also wanted to have this for the day that I got up the nerve to reach out to you. I'm glad you were a bigger person than me."

"I love you is all that matters."

She watched him open the album and on the first page were pictures of him and her during the time when they dated. As he flipped from one page to another, she could see the shock on his face when he saw page after page of pictures of him and underneath each one, she made sure to add the word, "Dada".

"Aiden loves books and I read to him every day and most nights after his bath. Then we pull out the photo album and I tell him how much he looks like his daddy and how much his daddy loves him and how much his mommy still loves his daddy," she said with tears in her eyes.

She knew that so much time had passed, but the love never faded and she didn't want to fight her truth. The reality broke her down and to know and hear that Preston still loves her despite what she'd done was something she would always cherish. How could she not still love him?

"Where did you get all of these pictures of us? I remember every one of them, but where did you get them?"

When he pointed to one of them with her in her cheerleader outfit, he laughed out loud.

"Remember that day? When I found out about the picture, I called you a stalker," she said.

"I snuck that picture when you weren't looking and made it my screen saver before I'd even approached you. I told you, I knew you would be my girl."

"Am I still?" she asked nervously. They had a lot more to talk about, but she put the stubborn part of her to rest and wanted to embrace whatever they could share together and not just because of Aiden, but because she never stopped loving him.

"Are you coming back to me? Can we try a relationship again? It's going to take work and I'm willing to do any and everything to make it work."

"From California?" she asked.

The timing wasn't good, but she had to know. What would a life with him be like with him living in Los Angeles and her and Aiden in Atlanta?

"Baby, distance wasn't the problem three years

ago. It was the fact that you didn't want to give it a try and see what a relationship would look like. For you, it was all or nothing. I never saw it that way, but I couldn't convince you. You shut me out and that was that, as far as you were concerned, but not for me. My heart was always going to belong to you. When was this?" he asked.

Sumaria looked over to see what picture he was referencing.

"That was when he realized he had feet. He would reach for them and tug on them with all of his might and then cry when it hurt. I had to get a picture of that. I know he didn't understand me, but I would tell him to let go of his own feet and he could stop crying. He would pull and pull. He is still fascinated with his own feet."

"What about this one?"

"I didn't have a big first birthday party for him. It was a party of four, me, mom, Tara and him. The minute I put the first cake for him to play in right in front of him, instead of reaching for it with his fingers or hand to test it, he just dropped his whole head in it. Your son is a comedian," she joked.

"So many pictures. Thanks for letting me see this. Looks like you captured every single day of his life. I can see him aging in each one. This is a lot."

There were specific pictures she wanted him to see.

"Turn a few more pages," he encouraged.

"Okay."

She watched him turn and turn and then he stopped. He saw them and she smiled.

"You have recent pictures of me?"

"I do and I can't lie – I printed them from your social media pages and other internet sites. I am so proud of you and I wanted Aiden to be proud of his daddy."

"Thank you for this. This album means so much to me."

"Take it with you; I have two of them. One is for Aiden and I was keeping this one for you. They have the exact same pictures in them."

"Are you serious? You did this for me?"

"Prez, I wanted you in Aiden's life from the start. I was stupid and I hope what I did won't live between us as a point of contention. It was the second biggest mistake I've ever made in my life."

"What was the first?"

She was on a roll with putting everything on the table and now was not the time to stop.

"Not holding onto what we had. You've missed out on so much and so have I."

"I don't want to miss anymore and I know you asked about California and I don't have an answer. I'm here now and I will be here for some time."

"Here as in Atlanta?"

"Yeah, I made some calls and I have some artists I need to work with on some new projects and my assistant is making some calls to get me some time in a studio here in Atlanta. I'm adding extended stay at my hotel until I have to fly out to a meeting or something else that I can't avoid, but I will be here. I want to see my son every day. I want to see you every day. I can't do that on the road."

"What about your work?"

"I have enough people working for me and making moves for me that I can get it done from here. Most important is my time with you and Aiden. Now I know why he didn't beat me up when he woke up and I was all in his face," he laughed. "He knew I was his daddy."

"Wait until he says, Dada. It's amazing that his first word was, Dada. I would point at your picture and say that every time we went through the book. I'm around him every day, Maria is here when I'm working, Tara is always around, of course and yet, the first time he speaks, he says, dada when I pointed to you in the book. He loves opening to a page with you on it to remind me that he knows you're his dada. It's the cutest thing."

"I don't know what to say. For days, I tried to rehearse what I would say to you and to keep my anger down and I find that I don't have any anger at all. I'm just happy I have him and hopefully you in my life. Can we start working on us?" he asked.

Sumaria bit her bottom lip in anticipation of her response, which she already had planted on her lips, but didn't want to seem too anxious in her response to him. Then she cursed herself for not revealing her true feelings immediately. Holding back is what caused her to lose him in the first place.

"Do you have a life in California? A woman? I mean, I've seen photos and videos of you with one woman or another. I'm not trying to pry, I'm just asking."

When he leaned back and looked her over from top to bottom and smiled, she knew he was feeling himself.

"Oh, you were secretly checking a brother out, huh? You know a lot about me. What else do you know?" he asked. "I'm just curious."

"I've kept up with you and your career and the parts of your personal life the media dug into. You'll see even more pictures in the album, but no pictures of you with women hanging all over you, though. I didn't like seeing that. I also know that for the upcoming award season, you're up for producer of the year, song of the year, which you wrote and the new artist of the year nomination is the hottest singer out these days and he's the first artist on the new label you and Anthony started months ago."

"You asked about women? What have you heard?"

He was fishing and she knew what he was trying to get her to say and she was ready to put it out there and be honest.

"You've been linked with some of the most beautiful women in Hollywood. I've seen pictures of you with dates to parties and other events and one particular one that seemed to show up in a lot of pictures and videos of you. Is that your girlfriend?" she asked.

"Inquiring minds want to know, huh? Her name is Ananda and we've been close. I haven't been a monk since we broke up, but as far as where my heart is, it's with you. Ananda knows all about you and that I have been and will always love you first. I've dated, had my fun, but nothing was ever serious and it never would be unless it was you. Sumaria, there never has been and never will be another woman for me other than you; never. I can't take my heart from you and give it to another woman. I don't have a girlfriend or any other significant other. Come here," he said.

No hesitation at all, she moved closer, leaning into his embrace.

"I can't believe after what I've done, you're so forgiving. I didn't expect that when I saw you at the cemetery."

"That's why you ran?" he asked.

"I was afraid and I needed to think. Tara tried to get me to think before I left, but I needed to be back in my comfort zone. I knew that you would eventually show up and soon. I needed a little time to gather my thoughts. I wasn't running away from you or trying to keep you from Aiden after you saw him that day. I needed a little space. Seeing you was unexpected and I wasn't prepared for the onslaught of emotions that I experienced."

"Emotions like what, other than fear?"

"It wasn't real fear – just the fact that I needed time

to process addressing Aiden with you and not knowing how you would react. When you walked away in the cemetery, I knew you were angry and I was afraid that I'd gone too far and that you would never forgive me for that."

"I need you closer," he whispered in her ear.

She knew what that mean. Years ago, when he said that, he wanted her in his lap so that he could hold her even closer. There were times when he would admit to her that he was lonely, all alone in the world except for her and he just needed to hold her. Shifting, she turned and slid onto his lap, straddling him with her legs on the outside of his, her ankles against his knees. They were face to face in an old intimate position that she'd never been in since him.

"How's this?" she asked, focusing all of her attention on his piercing gaze. In his eyes she once found peace and more love than any one person could take in. Looking at him now, nothing had changed. She saw home in his eyes.

"Perfect. Now, I have a question for you. Is there anyone keeping you warm at night or during the day? I know you said Hakeem was just a friend, but anyone else I need to find a place to hide his body?" he kidded.

She punched him playfully.

"I'm going to have to talk to Hakeem and it's not going to be pretty. He has shown interest in me for a long time and I told him once our business as attorney and client was over, I would go out with him. That business ended last week and then you showed up today. He doesn't know about our past or that you're Aiden's father."

"I got that. You're a woman every man would want. I don't blame him, but he's got nothing coming. I'm not trying to tell you what to do, but yeah, he's got nothing coming. Anyone else in your life on a more personal level?"

If Preston was cocky now, she can't begin to imagine what his reaction will be to what she was about to reveal.

"No one and there hasn't been anyone," she admitted.

Her words didn't sink right in from the look on his face. He didn't immediately respond, but instead, searched her face for an answer to the question in his head.

"You mean no one recently or are you saying no one at all."

She looked at him lovingly and tried to focus when all she could think about were how his big, strong hands were softly caressing the exposed skin on her legs. His touch was magical. He still had it and he could still get it and she couldn't wait to see his reaction when he found out no one else had ever gotten it.

"You're going to make me say it?"

"Say away, baby. Tell me."

She looked away out of embarrassment. What woman in her twenties who is single and has no sex life at all; zero."

"No one since you. No one before you and no one after you."

"What? Are you joking here to lighten the mood or to keep me from dying from a heart attack over another man making love to you or are you serious?"

"No one, Prez. You left and then I found out I was pregnant. Then I had Aiden and he's pretty much been my life outside of work and taking care of my parents. I dated some, but the idea of being with another man in that way crossed my mind, I would lose interest."

"Because of me?" he asked.

"Will your ego swell if I say yes?" she laughed and then went into his arms when he pulled her closer.

"No ego about anything between us. You did what you felt you needed and wanted to do for you. I can't say the same thing, but I can tell you that in my heart, there was only you. I know that men are different from women. We can separate what our body needs from what our heart needs and wants. Women are all from the heart and I respect that. It's been three years?"

She leaned back and saw the lust in his eyes and her body reacted to the radiating heat that fused through her. The fact that it had been three years since she'd had sex slammed into her and the only man she felt comfortable being that vulnerable with, to give herself to completely was now in her grasp. She felt an overwhelming need to do something about it.

There was a time when she would initiate making

love and felt free about getting her needs met without even saying a word. All it took was a look and he knew. When she looked in his eyes, she knew he saw it. Before she could tell him how much she wanted him, her words were halted by the sweet touch of his lips to hers.

His lips were hot, soft and moist and when she thought her mind would have taken her back to a time when they shared hot kisses in the past, it focused on the excitement that ran through her now and the erotic way his mouth loved on hers. When his arms went around and slid down her waist, she moved closer and her body hummed at the feel of him under her. She missed this; she missed him; she needed him. She needed to get back to the love that she let slip through her fingers, never to allow that to happen again.

"Do you have any idea how many nights I've dreamed of holding you like this again? I would reach out for you and you weren't there."

"I'm here now, Prez."

"What are you saying?"

"I don't know what I'm saying. I don't know what I'm thinking, but I do know that I miss your kisses. I miss you holding me like this and I miss..."

She let her words stop there. How could she ask a man she turned away from to take her back to a time when their love was wild and crazy and so was their lovemaking, something her body was clawing at her to speak up about.

"You miss? You don't have to say it. It hasn't been

that long and I remember what you look like when you need to feel me as close to you as I can get. Can I make love to you and have you figure out tomorrow if you want to throw me out or not?"

When he smiled with that look that she loved so much, she knew she couldn't deny him anything and she didn't want to because denying him would me she was denying herself.

"You'll have to carry me because I'm not sure my legs will work."

"Tired?" Preston asked standing with her in his arms.

"Knowing what's in store for me when we get to my bedroom? Not on your life. I'm unexpectedly wide awake after a busy day; I'm just weak in the knees. Even if I struggle with where we go from this day, my body is sure it wants you."

"You don't have to tell me more than once."

"I need to set the alarm."

Sumaria giggled as she pointed him in the direction of the control panel and with her still in his arms, he carried her to it where she entered the code and in the next second, he was taking the steps two at a time with her still in his arms. She rested her head and whispered a silent thanks that she didn't turn him away again.

9

Entering her bedroom, Preston lowered her to the bed which sat in the center of the room, up against a wall of red. The rest of the walls in the room were white. He took in the décor and hoped that this wouldn't be his only time in her space like this. The fact that her room was decorated in red and white, her favorite colors, did not surprise him one bit. He still remembered buying her all kinds of things in those colors back when they dated. She wore it all the time and every surface in her bedroom was covered in that color in some fashion.

He saw a fireplace on the wall in front of her bed where over top of it sat a large flat screen television. Under it was a soundbar.

"Do you have Bluetooth to the soundbar?" he asked.

"Yes."

"I want to turn on some music, but not too loud that it would wake Aiden, but then loud enough so that we don't wake Aiden. We have three years of making love to make up for and I intend to make sure you have me screaming your name!" he quipped.

She laughed as he lightened the mood and she gave him the code to connect his phone. Within minutes, slow music played from the speakers that were place in four corners around her room.

"Screaming my name, huh?" she asked.

When she started to remove her dress, Preston stopped her.

"Let me. I want to take in every part of your beauty. I need to see what I've been dreaming about, missing and most of all needing."

Moving to the bed where she was already sitting, Preston helped her slide back further, all the way to the top of the bed. He covered her body with his, unable to deal with a lot more talking; he only wanted to feel and have her feel him.

She had been like a temptress since the minute he saw her days ago in Meridian. He'd gone back to his hotel and images of her played over and over in his mind. He saw her at the event and damn near lost his mine he wanted her so bad. Now, to be here with her and to have her desiring him as she looked up at him from her position under him, he knew he had to have died and gone to heaven.

"I didn't want to admit it when I saw you, but when I left the cemetery, I didn't sleep all night. It wasn't because I was upset or bothered by the encounter, but it was because at that very second when you walked up to me, I wanted to jump in your arms and never leave them. I thought so much of a time when we would see each other again and what I would do. I did nothing that I dreamed about, but now, right now, this is what I have been thinking about and dreaming about."

"I love you, Sumaria. You don't have to say it and I don't need to hear it. I just needed you to hear me say it and know that I mean it. I never stopped and I never want to stop."

She started to respond, but couldn't when he reached up and caressed her shoulder before sliding the strap of her dress down one arm. When he reached for the other one, he didn't use his fingers, but he used his mouth. She watched every moment and the moment had her clutching her pearls or as some would say in more plain language, doing involuntary Kegel exercises. Until he satisfied her with what she really needed, where she needed it, she had to do that to calm the rise in hunger her body had for him.

As he kissed his way down her arms, she closed her eyes and enjoyed the feelings his hot tongue brought to the surface. It had been so long for her that she felt like a fresh fish out of the water, gasping for her next breath because every touch from him was stealing her breath away.

As her dress was being lowered from her body, she nearly leaped off the bed when it slid below her strapless bra covered breasts. When he used his tongue to kiss around the edge of the bra, just barely touching her flesh, she moaned out her pleasure and reached for him. She needed to feel him, she needed to feel his flesh inside of her, straining give her all that he was, all that he had to give. She leaned up enough for him to unclasp her bra and when the cups fell away, it was his hands that replaced where they had been. His fingers rolled her nipples between them as her hips moved in a circular motion, quietly begging for more.

"Damn, you are so beautiful and your breasts, always perfect and just for me. All for me, right?" he breathed against her ear.

"Mmm," was all she could muster up enough strength to do. Words escaped her.

"I need to hear it, baby. Just for me and for me only. Say it, baby," he whispered and this time, when his tongue caressed her ear, she was wild and crazy for him. That was her spot and he knew it; he remembered that. She also knew that until she answered him, he would continue to tease her and she needed him. She needed him like she needed to breathe to stay alive.

"Yes, only for you. No one else," she purred.

"That's what I like to hear."

When Preston leaned up to remove his shirt, she got her fill of just how he'd changed over the past few years. She knew his arms were muscled, but his chest was rock solid. He had to be spending a lot of time working out and it paid off. With his shirt off, he moved to the side of the bed and removed his pants and the boxer briefs he had on. By the time he rejoined her, he was in the buff and she could see it all. Something was new and her eyes, even in the dimly lit room, zeroed in on it. She let her fingers reach out to caress the area across his chest. He didn't that when she last saw him or she would have seen it. They made love in the middle of the day before he left and it was a bright, sunny day.

"You have a tattoo with my name on it? When did you do that? It's right over your heart."

"I did that about a year ago," he admitted.

"Preston, a year ago, we weren't together."

When he smiled at her, she melted and the thought that he would get a tattoo with her name on it even though they weren't together made her fall even deeper in love with him. Who does that?

"You were always going to be mine. You're still mine, right? I'm going to love you either way, but I just want to know what is really in your heart."

As he covered her body completely, she looked in his eyes and her loved spilled out from every fiber of her being.

"Yes, Prez. I am."

That was all Preston needed to hear. He couldn't wait another second to be inside of her. Though her dress was still down around her hips, he didn't care and he wasn't trying to take the time to remove it.

"You will always be mine; always be my heart. That's why your name is over my heart. I'm yours baby; always have been; always will be."

He then kissed her. Letting no more words keep him from joining them together and bringing them back to one.

He reached between them as they kissed wildly, passionately and slid her barely-there panties down her legs and tossed them out of the way. He fitted himself between her legs, pulling them up and around his hip. Raising his hips, he reached between them and found her soaking wet to his touch. She was there, she was ready and so was he. He hoped he would get the chance to be with her again and he would focus on foreplay at that time. Right now, he just needed to feel her wrapped tightly around him, milking him and taking any and everything from his body that she wanted and needed. No time like the present, he leaned forward, keeping their lips connected as he joined them together in the most intimate way possible. The minute he felt her wet folds surround him, he moved forward slowly, making sure he took the time to feel every part of him joining with every part of her. What he encountered was tightness and his mind went to the idea that she had never been with any other man. He was her one and only. Thinking about that alone was enough to already have his body on the brink of a powerful climax. Reigning in control, he took his time and loved her.

Sumaria didn't know what was coming over her. The moment Preston entered her body, all she knew was love. It was all around her, over her, beside her and most of all, inside of her. She needed this so bad, but only from Preston. No other man could ever make her feel this good or desire him this much. She locked her legs around his hips as he rode her, slow at first and when she lifted her hips to match him stroke for stroke, she knew he would increase the pace. As the sound of them making love wafted through the air in sound and in intensity, she held on to his shoulders as his lower half loved her while his mouth made love to her mouth. The kissing was erotic, sensual, amatory and it was everything she needed and then some. Her body was on another plane, in another time. She could feel herself rising to meet it.

When Preston pulled away from her mouth and rested his head on the pillow beside her head, in the crook of her neck, his moans brought her ecstasy. They loved madly and penetratingly and with titillating ease, her body shot off like a rocket and brought her to an orgasm so fast, that it was a welcoming shock to her system. She screamed through the ardent feeling and allowed her body to enjoy the pleasure of being loved so completely.

Preston's breaths grew louder and louder, his panting seared through her body as the movement of his hips increased. She freed his body from the grasp of her legs to allow him body to get as wild as he wanted to get and that's what he did. When he leaned up and locked eyes with her in the heat of the moment, she saw the moment his release poured over him like a tumultuous wave. She saw it in his eyes, knowing he didn't want to look away and she felt it in the way his body surged into hers with so much love and deliberate passion that she wanted to do nothing other than encourage him on. This was a moment they both had been yearning for and though there had been years in between this love and the last time they loved, being with him felt like home.

Preston couldn't take his eyes off of her. He didn't want to say that times when he had been with other women, he only reached completion when he closed his eyes and imagined her. He no longer had to do that. His love was right in front of him and he would never close his eyes again when he made love to her. He wanted to see everything about her at their most intimate time.

"I love you, baby," he groaned out and then he left his release have control as he bucked wildly above her. He heard the bed hitting the wall and though he didn't want to wake their sleeping son, he couldn't control how grateful he was that he was with her once again, the place he had been trying to get back to. Now that he was here, he wanted to do everything in his power to stay here.

He rode out his release until his body began to calm. His breathing was so erratic, he struggled to catch his breath. When Sumaria reached up and caressed his chest, kissing his tattoo of her name, he felt tears in his eyes. He's wanted this day for such a long time and now that he was here, he couldn't contain his emotions.

He kissed her again and again and again and when he thought that her lips could be raw from all of his powerful kisses, he kissed her again. He never wanted her to forget this exact moment when she welcomed him back into her life and into her body.

"Are you alright?" he asked when he could find enough breath to speak.

"I'm better than alright."

"Worth the three year wait?" he asked, rolling to the side to take his weight from the top of her body. He pulled her with him, not wanting her to be too far away from him.

"More than that. The question is, will I have to wait another three years?" she asked humorously.

Preston pulled her so that she now rested on top of his body.

"I'll give you three minutes and you can have as much of me as you want."

Sumaria felt his readiness between them, growing long and hard against her stomach. She moaned at the thought that they had all night.

"I'm willing our son to stay asleep and I hope you're not planning on sleeping tonight. You have a lot of time to make up for," she jested.

Preston turned so that they were facing each other and he slid her dress off of her body.

"I say let's get it in where we can and hopefully, that will be all night," he said.

"Let me start," Sumaria said and then proceeded to show him exactly what she meant as she slid further down the bed to that part of him that stood at attention waiting to get even more reacquainted with her.

~~

Preston heard crying and leaped out of bed. He was usually a heavy sleeper and thought about how that had now changed. He was more than aware that his ears were keen for listening out for his son.

"Pants," Sumaria groggily called out to him from the bed.

Looking down at his nakedness, he shook his head and grabbed his pants. She'd put it on him so good through the night that he was forgetting his pants.

"Aiden definitely would have screamed for you seeing me walk into his room like this," he joked.

"I can get him."

"I want to get him. I'll be right back."

As Aiden's cries grew louder, he hurried over to his crib.

"Hey! What's with all this noise this early in the morning?"

He went to lift Aiden up and he stopped crying and started giggling.

"Dada, dada, dada," he said and Preston could feel his own heart in his chest swell.

"Dada is right and I love you. Let's go see mommy," he said, hugging him closer and, bouncing him as they walked into the bedroom where Sumaria was already up and moving around. He sat down on the bed and bounced Aiden on his lap. When he broke out into a fit of laughter, his day was officially made.

"Good morning, my sunshine," Sumaria said when Aiden reached for her.

"He called me dada! I picked him up and he called me dada, like three times in a row."

"Well, aren't you excited. I told you he knew you and any minute now, he's going to be wondering why he's not eating his morning fruit. I'll go get that together while you entertain him."

"Sumaria, this is good. You know that, right? I haven't been this happy in a very long time. Are we good? I know last night was intense and not planned and neither was the lack of protection which I now know we didn't use. I'm good on that end, just so you know. The only woman I've ever been with without any kind of protection is you and even that was only a few times."

She walked toward him and leaned down and he joyously accepted the kiss she planted on him. They all laughed when Aiden grabbed her by the hair and joined in the moment by kissing her on the cheek.

"I guess that kiss just sealed everything for me and for our son and yes, I got caught up in being with you again and it happened. I will tell you that there was no kind of protection in place against us making another one of him last night; all night and even earlier this morning. Remember, I haven't been with anyone so there was no need to have any in place."

"I'm not mad about what could happen after every single time we went there. Are you?" he asked, choosing his words carefully with Aiden in the room.

"Not one iota."

"We are in this together, baby. Know that I am all in, one hundred percent."

"Well, if something does come out of it, you'll get your first-hand experience at child birth."

"That's even better. I'll keep an eye on this little guy while you make his breakfast and then while he's eating, I can make you breakfast."

"Cook for me?"

"I've learned a few things in three years," he said.

"Yes. Yes, you have and my body thanks you for that ocean that now replaces my drought."

Preston laughed so hard that Aiden looked at him startled and then laughed along with him as if he knew what they were laughing at.

"I do what I can do, when I can do it and you know that I will. What are your plans for today? Do you have to go into work? I can keep an eye on him today if you need me to or if you want me out of your hair for a while, I can come back later."

"I love having you here and I'm off today. Tara is getting the showroom back in order for the next couple of days and we'll open back up on Monday. It's the weekend and I was planning on hanging around here."

"If you have things to do, I understand. I know your

life can't be placed on hold because we're back together. I know you won't leave and not come back."

"Jokes?" he surmised.

"Yeah, I had to get that one it. It was itching to come out."

"Any other itches?" he asked.

"This afternoon when Aiden takes his nap, I hope you'll be around for the scratch-fest."

"Baby, I'm not going anywhere. So, my favorite song will now be, Baby Come Back? You're officially taking me back?" he asked.

"I am just as much as you are taking me back. That song plays both ways for us. One thing. I need to talk to Hakeem. He deserves an explanation of what he walked in on yesterday. I promise you I was not involved with him, but he did ask me out and I did say yes."

"Is he level-headed or will he be trouble?"

Preston remembered the way Hakeem looked at her when he walked over to them and interrupted them talking. He knew the look of a man in love and now that he knew nothing developed between them, he was concerned that Hakeem wouldn't take her backing up on giving him a chance as lightly as she probably thinks he will.

"I don't think there's a problem. I just looked at my phone and he's called a few times and sent a couple of messages asking if we can talk today. You good with that?" she asked.

"I am if you are. I'd like to be around."

"Okay."

She hesitated at the door. He knew she had more to say, but didn't.

"Tell me," he said. "You're keeping something from me. What is it? I saw it all over your face."

She walked back over to the bed and sat down where Aiden climbed into her lap.

"He sent a text last night that I didn't read until this morning."

"And it said?"

"That he could see that I was busy and he assumed the unknown car at my house was you."

Preston tried to hold back his concern. The guy must have come by her house. How else would he know there was a car at her house? He kept a smile on his face since Aiden was looking right at him.

"He drove by here last night? Did he say when?"

"No, just that he saw the car and drove off. He needed to talk to me."

"And you think that's level-headed? He's in love with you. Did you know that?"

"But we aren't dating. I agreed to have dinner with him after everything with the event died down, but I'm not doing that now. He saw us kissing. He knows there is you. He just doesn't know the full extent. When I tell him, he'll understand that I wasn't being secretive. I never stopped loving you and I want us to work."

"Still, do not talk to him without me around. I

would say do it by phone, but that would be rude. You should invite him here later today and we can talk to him together. I don't want him walking away thinking you were playing him. I know how guys can be. I need to be able to read his response to know if he's going to be trouble or not."

"Trouble? What kind of trouble?"

"The kind from a man who's in love and is rejected. I'm going to go to my hotel to shower and change and I'll be back. Don't have him over here until I get back."

"Okay. How long are you staying at this hotel?" she asked.

"Until I figure out how we're going to do this. I don't want to be a text, phone call, video chat kind of man in your life or in my son's life. I'll figure it out. The hotel is an indefinite place for me to stay for as long as I need to."

"You can stay here with us if you want to. I know it's only been a day and things are moving pretty fast, but Aiden would love to see you every day and I know I would. There is plenty of room if you start to feel crowded and an office if you need to handle any business."

"Are you sure? Don't offer a brother the prize and then snatch it away when you realize you didn't really mean it."

"I mean it and it's up to you. Just know that we would love to have you here while we figure out how to do this."

"I'll check out when I get there and bring my stuff back. I don't have much, but I plan to have a few things sent here from my place in L.A. You good with that?"

"I love you, Prez. This is how it should be."

"Apple," Aiden said.

"See, told you. That boy loves his fruit. He has it every morning while I figure out what else to make him. Have fun bonding with him and bring him down in a few to eat."

"I love you, Sumaria."

"It's a good thing," she quipped and left the room.

"Okay, buddy. It's you and me. What are we going to get into while your mommy is making you breakfast? Wait, I know. Let's look at the picture book and then we can take pictures of me and you to add to it. How's that? Yes?"

"Yes," Aiden said.

He didn't know if Aiden understood what he was saying yes to, but he picked him up and headed back to his room to find the other book Sumaria said she kept. He would worry later about how they would deal with Hakeem. Unlike Sumaria, he saw the look in Hakeem's eyes and it wasn't just shock, he was vengeful.

10

The atmosphere in her house was different. Preston had just left out to go gather his things back at the hotel, telling her he wouldn't be long. He'd stayed around playing with Aiden until it was time for his nap. He wanted to put him down and then get back before he woke up. She loved how Preston didn't want to miss any part of Aiden's life. She never should have let this much time go by, but thankfully he was forgiving and taught her a lot about being just as forgiving. As she moved between the kitchen and the family room cleaning up the mayhem left by Aiden who took great pleasure in showing Preston all of his toys, her phone vibrated on the kitchen counter. Looking at it, there was a message from Hakeem and what he said had her on edge. She read it to herself and then read it out loud.

"I see your guest just left. Can I come in and talk? I want to talk about us and our dinner date we still need to schedule. I was thinking about dinner tomorrow night, somewhere nice? Can you come to the door and let me in?"

His message gave her chills. Hakeem was sitting outside her house someplace in a spot where he could see that Preston had just left. What should she do? Preston wanted to be here when she talked to Hakeem. Her plan was to call him on Sunday and explain everything and to let him know that there would be no future relationship for them. How creepy was it that he drove by her house last night and then today, he's sitting out there again? Had he been there all night?

She dropped her phone to the floor when the front doorbell rang. Looking at the screen on the kitchen wall that was connected to the camera outside her front door, she saw Hakeem. He was dressed in a brown sweat suit, so he'd gone home at some point. Why was he hanging around outside and why wait until after Preston left? She walked slowly toward the door and stopped when he kept pushing the doorbell without letting up. He then went from ringing the bell to knocking on the door, but not like a normal person – he was knocking without stopping in between. All of a sudden, she felt terrorized when she heard his knock on the large bay window of her living room. He'd gone from knocking on the door to now knocking on the window? What was up with him.

"Sumaria? Are you in there? You didn't leave with Prez so you must still be here. I just want to talk to you for a few minutes. We need to set up our dinner date. Remember, we're involved now. I'm not your lawyer anymore and we're supposed to have dinner. Can I come in? Can you hear me?"

Her motherly instinct set in and without going anywhere near the door, she ran up the stairs and stood outside of Aiden's room where he was sleeping and she dialed Preston. She barely got all the numbers pushed because her hands wouldn't stop shaking.

She expelled the breath she was holding the minute Preston answered and she screamed his name, not meaning to scare him, but out of relief and sheer terror.

"Sumaria? What's wrong? Is something wrong with Aiden?" he asked.

"No, no! Hakeem is here. He's ringing the bell, calling my phone over and over, knocking on the door and even knocking on the window asking me to let him in to talk about a dinner date. I didn't know what to do. He sent a text right after you left saying he saw you leave. He must have been somewhere outside my house watching. I'm scared."

She heard what sounded like racecar wheels peeling on street. Preston must have turned back toward her.

"I'm only a few blocks away. Where are you and where is Aiden?" he asked.

"He's asleep and I'm outside of his room."

"Is the alarm on? Did you set it after I left?"

"It is."

"Is there another way into your house that's not alarmed?"

"No. Should I call the police? He's really banging now and going between banging and ringing the bell and it's getting louder. He's going to wake Aiden.

"No. I got this covered. I don't care what you hear or what you see, do not take the alarm off or come out of the house. Do you understand? Stay with Aiden. I'll got this."

"Pres, no. What are you going to do? You said he may not be level-headed."

"Don't worry about me. I'm a man and I saw it. I saw the look in his eyes when he caught us kissing. I'm pulling up right now. Hang up and stay up there with Aiden. I'll call you. Do not come out here."

She hung up, went into Aiden's room and sat on the floor next to his crib and waited.

~~

Preston pulled up to the house and barely had a chance to turn his car off before he was out of it and rushing up to Hakeem. He held his hands up to not seem too aggressive. He didn't want a scene, but he wasn't going to let Hakeem think that his presence was welcomed.

"What are you doing, man?" he asked Hakeem who looked surprised to see him.

"I'm not doing anything. I wanted to talk to Sumaria about some stuff regarding her contracts."

"You couldn't call her on the phone? It's Saturday

and she's enjoying a day off."

From Hakeem's body language, he was getting riled up and he probably wasn't ready to listen to any reasoning. There was a madness to his facial expression and then ire.

"You were here. It being Saturday didn't prevent you from being here. Was it an all-nighter?" Hakeem asked, putting him off.

"And that means?"

"Nothing. Look, I'm not bothering anyone. I'm her attorney and I have business with her."

"Yeah? Well, she called me saying she was afraid because you were ringing her bell, banging on the door and her window and when I pulled up, you were literally trying to see in the window. I think by now, if she wanted to talk to you, she would have responded. You should probably leave."

A man without common sense was standing before him. Hakeem was rocking from side to side, first with his arms crossed and now he'd locked his fingers behind his back – still rocking. He warned Sumaria that Hakeem was off and now he's seeing it for himself.

"Oh, should I? Why? So that you can slide in on her? Did she tell you that we're involved or about to be?"

Preston didn't want to make light of how Hakeem felt, but his impression of what was going on was different what Sumaria said was happening.

"I don't think that's the reality, bruh."

He backed up when Hakeem began stomping in place. What the hell? He was glad Sumaria had called him. The guy was a loose cannon.

"And you know the reality? What's going on with you and Sumaria? I saw you kissing her and it didn't look like the first time you've kissed. You've been seeing her behind my back?"

"She and I have history and it's not behind your back. You're not involved with her."

Remaining calm was the name of the game. This is why he rarely traveled without his security team. He was used to being accosted by fans and crazy ass women who thought that because they knew his name, they were involved with him. He was trying to be patient with Hakeem, but he also would grab his phone in a second to call the police if need be. He was trying to dissolve any situation since this was Sumaria's home and her neighborhood.

"Oh? She didn't tell me anything about that when I asked her to go out with me and she agreed. How long ago was this history because I've been interested in her for quite some time and she never mentioned you. You would think someone as well-known as you would have come up in a conversation between me and her."

"None of that matters. All you need to know is that you should move on. She's not going to be going out with you or entertaining being involved with you and you should probably think before you make another visit here. You're a lawyer, you know the repercussions of being someplace where you're not invited."

"I'm her lawyer!"

"Hakeem, you were her lawyer. As of today, I think she'll be seeking other counsel that doesn't have a personal interest."

"Why? Are you planning on being around all the time? Don't you live in Los Angeles? Why are you here? What? So you spent the night with her. I don't care. This is between me and Sumaria. You've had your playboy fun."

Preston was done talking as he moved closer to Hakeem. He was ready just in case something jumped off. Being from the streets and spending years taking care of himself, some bumpy lawyer in a sweat suit wouldn't deter him.

"Hakeem, I'm asking you nicely to walk away. She was going to reach out to you to let you know that whatever interest you had in her had to be directed elsewhere."

"Ah, so you're involved with her? You spend the night and she's your woman?"

"No. Look, man to man, I don't want any trouble with you, but I'm telling you that you need to walk away, man. I am involved with her. Like I said, we have history that goes back a lot of years and I'm not going anywhere. She's my woman and Aiden is my son."

He said it out loud to someone else other than Anthony and Sumaria and the words were music to his ears.

"Son? Aiden is your son? What because you're claiming her, you're now claiming her son as yours? Get out of here with that. That Hollywood lifestyle of everything you want being yours has gone to your head."

"Hakeem, I am Aiden's father; his biological father. She and I are going to make our family work and that's why I'm telling you to go ahead and walk away and stop frightening her. She's in there scared. I know you care about her, but this isn't it. You say you know about me, then you also know that I'm not going to leave here as if I don't see you standing here on the borderline of harassing her. She's not interested and you're trespassing. Any good lawyer knows what that means. I don't want to blow this up and make any trouble for you, legally or any other way. Do a solid here and leave Sumaria alone. I won't warn you a second time and before you ask if I'm threatening you, damn right I am. Are we clear here?"

Preston waited. He was ready for whatever Hakeem was going to bring his way. The man was practically stalking Sumaria and he wasn't about to let anything happen to her.

"You're really his father? Aiden's?"

"I am. I'm not moving in on a woman you thought could be yours. The timing just sucks and she doesn't mean to hurt you behind giving you hope. I'm a man who wants my family back and I'm here to stay. Now, you could continue down this path and it won't turn out well for you. I'm talking to you like a man who loves her and my son. There is nothing for you here."

He saw Hakeem open his mouth to respond and then shut it back just when he turned and started walking away.

"Tell Sumaria I'm sorry and that I hope this doesn't meant that she'll take her business from the firm. Her case has already been assigned to someone else. I hear you and I didn't know he was your son. She never told me who his father was and I never asked. A son should have his father in his life. I'm a fan and I saw the interviews where you talked about your life growing up and what it was like to not have your father in your life. I wouldn't want to come between a man and his son. You still love her?" Hakeem asked.

"More than my life."

Hakeem didn't say anything else. He walked over to his car, got in and drove away. When his car was out of sight, he took out his phone and called Sumaria.

"What's happening?" she asked before he could get a word out.

"Nothing. We talked man to man and he understands that he doesn't have a chance. Come open the door and let me in. I'm going to park back along the garage."

"I thought you needed to change and check-out from the hotel? I didn't mean to bring you into this mess. He surprised me with this behavior."

"You couldn't know because you were at the

beginning of what he thought was going to be a relationship. I'm still going to check out, but I don't want to leave right now. I'll reach out to my assistant and have all that taken care of, including having my things brought here to your house. I don't want to hover, but I want to stay close for today. I love you, baby."

"Thanks for coming back for me; again," she said.

"I'll always be here, now come let me in. I'm thinking when Aiden is up from his nap, let's go out and have dinner. Can you believe that I can finally take my woman out for a nice dinner and not have to worry about if I can pay my rent after?"

Preston disconnected the call and put his phone in his pocket the minute the front door opened and behind it stood the woman he worked hard to get back to and his son, who was wide awake and reaching for him.

"He had a little cat nap and needs you to put him back to sleep."

"I'm always down for that. Let me move my car before more of your neighbors wonder why it's parked crazy in the middle of the street."

"Okay, give me him and you do that while I put some clothes on. Lunch out somewhere sounds nice. Say, ever been to the zoo?" Sumaria asked.

"Never, not even once."

"Good. Aiden and I want to take you to our favorite place. It's a zoo and aquarium in one."

"Baby, I'm open to going anywhere and doing anything you want. Do you know what I really want to do?"

"No."

"Take you and Aiden on a vacation someplace. All I've been doing is work and then more work. I want to have some time away with just the three of us while we talk about our future."

"I'm going anywhere you go. I'm ready to do that because you came back for me. I want to now go everywhere with you."

Jogging to his car, he looked at the two most important people in his life. He couldn't wait to introduce them to the world.

Epilogue
Six Months Later

"I now pronounce you husband and wife. You may kiss your bride!"

Preston didn't just lean down to kiss Sumaria to seal their love as husband and wife. He picked her up in his arms and kissed her with the deep love and affection all men should have for the woman they loved as much as he loved her. It wasn't until the preacher tapped him on the arm and their guests began to laugh out loud that he finally let go of her lips and set her back down on her feet.

"I guess I need to save something for later," he said against her lips.

When Aiden tugged on his pant leg, he leaned down and scooped him up in his arms.

"Twins in looks and attire!" Sumaria beamed.

"Who knew they had Armani tuxedos for little guys," Preston boasted.

When the music played, they turned around to the cheers of over two hundred guests at their June wedding at the St. Regis Hotel in Atlanta and walked down the aisle to their private suite just outside of the reception area where they were going to provide a six-course meal and entertainment from some of the industry's biggest singers, thanks to the connections he'd made in the past few years. His best friend and best man, Anthony was about to take the stage, but before then, he needed some alone time with his new bride and Aiden who was having a good time playing dress up in his own tuxedo and patent leather shoes.

Closing the door behind them, he did get the kiss he was trying to lay on her after the preacher pronounced them man and wife, but this time, he wouldn't have to stop because there was an audience.

This time, there would be no interruptions as she melted in his arms, wrapped her arms around his neck and held on. She would need to because the minute he caressed her lips and the ideal that she was now his wife fused through him, he didn't hold back. He kissed her with everything in him. He poured years of missing her and needing her into the lustful connection and only when Aiden pushed his way between them did he move away.

"Okay, okay, I got it," he said to him.

"Today was perfect," Sumaria said.

"You are perfect and you've made me a very happy man. Nothing in life could compare to what today means," he declared.

"You have added new meaning to starting from the bottom and now you're here. I don't know if I've told you how very proud of you I am and today is another thing to add to that list. You made this happen and I love you so much for it. I know I haven't always appreciated the sacrifices you've made for our love, but I'm glad you did."

"And you're sure you have no issues with us making our home base in Los Angeles? I know how hard you've worked to build your brand here in Atlanta."

"I'm perfectly sure. Where you are is where Aiden and I need to be. Yes, I got that we could make it work with many frequent flyer miles, but I don't want that and besides, it's time I let Tara take over the operation here in Atlanta. She's knows just as much about set design as I do and truth be told, she was a big part of why I got the contract to do the set design for those new Atlanta reality shows. I wouldn't pass up the opportunity to go into business with my husband."

"You know I can't wait for that. The video shoots for our artists could use some help. Me and Anthony are signing four new artists and marketing will be key once we get their mega hits written."

"Though, I am questioning living in your condo. That was fine when me and Aiden were flying out to visit you over the past few months, but to live in, isn't going to work. I want him to have space to play outside in a big back yard with a jungle gym and definitely a swimming pool. We will be in bright, sunny California."

"Baby, I'm going to leave that up to you. I'm going to live in whatever you pick out or build and I already know the design inside is going to be magazine, front cover worthy. I've waited for what seems an eternity to have a life with you, one I know we are building together."

"Years ago, you did promise me a life in California. We need to get to the reception because as much as I love Atlanta, I'm so ready to get back to Los Angeles."

"What about a honeymoon? You still haven't told me where you want to go so that I can make some secret arrangements."

"I need to talk to Tara about keeping Aiden for us. Maria will help her, but I need to work that out before we jet off to someplace exotic."

"Without my son? No way, he comes with us and we'll bring help along. Maria has already agreed to move to the west coast to keep looking after Aiden. She's coming out in what, two or three months after she settles her affairs here in Atlanta?"

"You want to take a three-year-old with us on our honeymoon?"

"Baby, I'm not going anywhere without my son for a while. I can hire any and everyone to travel with us, but I need him close."

Sumaria stopped him from talking in the best way she knew how; she leaned up and kissed his perfect lips. She could see him getting anxious over the idea of leaving the country without Aiden. She wouldn't dare do that if he was set on taking him with them. She loved the idea of taking Aiden with them.

"Okay, I was about to go overboard, right?" Preston exclaimed.

"You were getting all hyped up as if I was giving our son away. I got that you feel some type of way when you're away from him and I understand it. I don't want a whole lot of people looking after him, so I'll check with Maria and we'll get something planned. You have two big press conferences coming up, one about your nomination for producer of the year and the other with your artist who is being labeled the breakout artist of the year with his new artist nomination. We don't have to do a honeymoon right now because every day together is a honeymoon. I want to make sure when we go, there will be no distractions. How's that?"

Preston knew he needed to relax. Ever since he found out about Aiden and have since developed the strongest bond with him, every minute with him is precious and if he's more than a day or two away from him, he doesn't feel right.

"I hear you, baby and thank you. I know I can be extra when it comes to him and a little obsessive when it comes to spending time with him. I want a nice, long honeymoon and respite from anything related to work and for the length of time I want to be away as a family, it needs to be all three of us."

"You mean, all four of us right? Don't forget about this little one. I'm only two months along, but we are still a family of four now."

Preston stooped down on one knee, placed his hand on her belly through her white Vera Wang, diamond encrusted wedding dress and kissed his child growing in her womb.

"I can't wait to meet you."

"Girl or boy?" Sumaria asked.

He looked up at her and chuckled when Aiden ran over and hopped on his back. That was a game they played often when Aiden wanted a ride on his back. He would stoop and Aiden would hop on. Not willing to tell him he wasn't stooping for that reason, he held him tight on his back and stood.

"What?" he asked her.

"Do you want a girl or a boy this time?"

Pulling her close as he held Aiden on his back, he looked to the side and noticed they were standing in front of a floor to ceiling mirror. What he was looking at was what he'd always desired; a family of his own to love and cherish and now that he had what he never wanted to let go of, he was happy with whatever came his way.

"As long as we're a family, I'm take either or even both. Hell, I'm thinking two more of each and I want to always be there from beginning to forever with you."

When she turned and leaned into his chest, Preston held them both closely.

"Then let's go get this party started. We have a hall full of people wondering where we are."

"Stay close?" he asked.

"Always and forever."

Unforgettable

Baltimorean Reagan Kelly was expecting an uneventful weekend in New York City visiting her sister between Thanksgiving and Christmas. Though in the holiday spirit, the last thing she thought she'd find on a cold, wintery night was a chance at romance.

Two days in New York City for business and a chance to see his best friend was all Crime Novelist, Keith Jackson had time for, or so he thought. He soon found time to extend his stay when the chance of a lifetime to spend four incredible days with the most beautiful woman he'd ever encountered landed at his feet.

An unforgettable weekend is one thing, but can that weekend turn into a lifetime of unconditional love for Reagan and Keith, two self-professed workaholics, who didn't have a reason to slow down and smell the roses until now?

When I Think of You

Leo Westmoreland is an ordinary guy living in Harlem, New York, working three jobs to make ends meet the best way he can in order to take care of his family years after his abusive father disappeared from their lives. He's kept romance on the back burner, but that's all about to change.

Raquel Johnson was born with a silver spoon in her mouth to a father who owns one of the top money management firms in Manhattan. Though she's never wanted for anything, she's made her own achievements in life and now sits as an executive with his company. Her dating life has consisted of men who value money, power and prestige over unconditional love, the one thing she desires the most.

Leo and Raquel meet and share a connection that breathes new life into them and proves that focusing on each other and the love they can have together is more important than anything else.

Black Love

Dawson Frazier stood on the sideline and watched the woman of his dreams get mistreated and disrespected by his philandering best friend, the man she was about to marry. He wanted to step in and rescue her, but he didn't want her coming to him that way.

Riley Cooper was left at the altar, confused and embarrassed by the man she thought loved her. It took her over a year to get over that disappointment and with the help of a good man, she was able to see what it really meant to love and to be loved.

About the Author

Cheryl Barton lives in Maryland and in her spare time she loves to read espionage, crime and romance novels, cook, watch Sci-fi movies, spend time with family and friends and enjoy Maryland steamed crabs. Cheryl is celebrating 30 years as a government employee and loves writing romance novels when she's not working. Cheryl is the author of 31 romance novels, 3 inspirational novels and is proud of 4 book compilation projects with several other incredible women called, "One Sister Away: Encouraging Words from One Sister to Another" – a series of books meant to encourage, empower and inspire other women. People often ask Cheryl which book is her favorite of all of those she's written. While she finds it hard to select one favorite, Cheryl still looks to her first novel, Bachelor Not for Sale, if she had to pick a favorite because it was her first novel and the one that inspired her to continue writing.

Cheryl was a 2019 Finalist for the Emma Award given by Romance Slam Jam and a 2018 Finalist for the Literary Trailblazer of the Year award by the Indie Author Legacy Award. Cheryl is a member of the Romance Writers of America – National Chapter, the Maryland Romance Writers and the Contemporary Romance Writers groups, the Black Writers' Guild of Maryland and the International Women Writers Guild.

Connect with Cheryl Barton

www.cherylbarton.net
www.crbarton.com
www.amazon.com/author/cherylbarton

Instagram: @cherylbartonbooks
Twitter: @cbartonbooks
Facebook: @cherylbartonbooks